A Poor Excuse for a Book

About the Author

Nathan J. McDougal is a relatively unknown author of some mediocre skill. *A Poor Excuse for a Book* is his first published work. The first of what he hopes to be many, many more.

A Poor Excuse for a Book

A collection of short stories

Nathan J. McDougal

Last Legend Publishing

First Edition April 2019

Book design by Nathan McDougal

ISBN 978-1-7337999-1-1 (paperback)
ISBN 978-1-7337999-0-4 (ebook)
LCCN   2019902722

www.nathanjmcdougal.com
www.lastlegendpublishing.com

This book is dedicated to Marsha, Ethan and Naomi.

A special thank you to my mother, my father, my brother and my sister and to all of my family and all of my friends.

We did it.

Author's Note: I'll keep this short. The first part of this book is true. The short stories are real stories from my real life as I remember them. It all happened just as described as best as I can remember, unless of course this book is being used against me in a court of law for whatever odd reason, if that's the case, none of it's true and I made it all up. Otherwise, yeah its real.

The second part of this book is purely fictional. That's it. Part one really happened and part two is make believe. Keep that in mind and above all else, enjoy.

Table of Contents

PART I: THE NONFICTION

<u>Ignorance is Bliss</u>

I found a dead body once...

When I was around 4 years old, I was jumping on a bed when my mother caught me in mid-jump, sat me down on the edge of the bed and begin to put shoes on my feet. She told me we were going to see my grandfather, my father's father, and as I remember, I was fairly excited.

My existence started at that moment. Which is to say, it is the earliest memory I have had for as long as I can remember. Four years of age, jumping up and down on my mother's bed in our little government assisted housing unit in the projects, my conscious mind came into being. I have no recollection of life before that particular point in time.

After that first event, my memory is more of a medley of random happenings that I sometimes get confused with really good episodes of my favorite television shows. And then, there are other things. The unmistakable things that kind of happen to you, around you and within you, all at once. Things that serve as a type of memory buoy system to help you maintain a chronological sense of direction in ocean like mass that is your living memory. Memory markers I'd call them. They are not always tragic or even sad really, they simply are.

For me, one such event occurred around the age of seven or eight. As I recall I was at my aunt's house. She lived in Preston Taylor, a public housing development on the west side of Nashville. My aunt's house was only a few buildings from where my mother and I had lived a few years earlier. A stone's throw from the scene of the oldest memory my consciousness could access. It was a warm summer night, and for some reason beyond my knowledge there was a blackout in the neighborhood, and everyone in the house was now out on the front porch. Of course, me being an eight-year-old boy, I picked the perfect time to have to use the bathroom. And of course, me being an eight-year-old boy the simple solution was for me to go around to the back of the building. Now peeing on the side of a building posed no problem for me, as a matter of fact, I feel no boy can truly become a man until he has taken a whiz in the open air. It's a rite of passage, common practice in those days for boys my age. I stepped off the porch and walked around to the back, alone and in the dark.

The corpse was lying there, on the ground some 15 feet from the back of the building. There was no blood, no gore, just a human body, limp and lifeless lying still in the grass behind my aunt's project building. It was a man, black and young, probably 19 or 20 years old. His head was shaved bald, and he wore a black hooded sweatshirt. He was on his back, with both his mouth and eyes open wide. His expression even now is still vivid in my mind, it was like that of a human machine that someone had switched into "off" mode. He stared up past a starless night sky, his face void and emotionless. His eyes bulged, but only slightly, not in a manner that was grotesque or graphic, but simply, in a way that was unnatural and uncommon. His mouth lay open just as wide as his eyes. He looked as if he were choking, but there was no desperate struggle for breath, no panicked gasps for air and oxygen, only silence and stillness. It was dark out, and the artificial light from the street lamps and apartment windows was absent, but the moon shone down and illuminated the body with an eerie perfection that allowed me to take in every necessary detail.

My first instinct was not that he was dead. I tried to talk to him, the entire time keeping my distance, speaking in low whisper, then eventually graduating to "Hey!" in a voice much deeper than my own, all in an attempt to disguise my age and fear; all in an effort to elicit some type of response, but to no avail. Yet, regardless of the morbid situation, I had to 'go,' and with a corpse a few feet away, I did. I turned my back to the body so that I was facing the building as I relieved myself. The entire time, peering back over my shoulder at the deceased, praying that he didn't jump up and grab my leg. I only had to pee, but if someone had even said, "Boo!" I would have instantly shat my pants. I was terrified, but not for the reasons you would expect. It wasn't the body that scared me. It was not the lingering presence of fresh death that made me uneasy, but rather, it was the anticipation of being frightened by some unimagined surprise element while in the midst of emptying my bladder, that made me nervous. I finished my business as quickly as I could and rushed back around to the front of the building.

Back on the front porch, I sat down and proceeded not to utter a single word about what I had just seen. Not only did I not mention seeing a dead body I had somehow become completely oblivious to the fact that I had just come from an undiscovered crime scene. As a matter of fact, I came back and resumed whatever conversation I was having before I had to excuse myself. There was no shock. No one in my family thought I was acting strangely. I did not look like I had just seen a ghost, which is odd because I should have. I should have peed my pants. Instead, I just peed and then went on about my night as if nothing extremely out of the ordinary had just taken place.

Now to be honest with you, I am not sure why I didn't say anything. I just know once I got back around the building, I was fine. I was seemingly and completely unaffected by what I had witnessed. In my 8-year-old priorities of concern, stumbling across dead bodies was simply, not a big deal. I can only assume that my mind was too young to truly grasp what I had seen and that I was somehow shielded by both my ignorance and my innocence.

My Father the Artist

Young boys idolize their Fathers, and I am no an exception to this rule. As a matter of fact, I may very well be the epitome of it.

My father is an artist, and by that, I mean, he can draw. He can draw really well actually. I'm not sure if that explains or is the reason for, my love of comic books, cartoons and all things fantasy and fiction. I just know, as a kid, having a dad that could draw all the characters that I loved felt like having a dad with a superpower. His talent fed my imagination.

I mean this guy was a real artist, he had a drafting table and everything. You know what a drafting table is right? It's like a desk that sits at an angle. I think it's designed, so you are not drawing on a completely horizontal surface. Maybe it's supposed to be easier on your back or something. I don't know the details. I just know, to this day, you don't see a guy with a drafting table unless he knows what he's doing.

I remember I use to watch him draw. What comes to mind at this particular moment, is a very specific memory of him drawing a picture of Spider-Man. Now, what was distinctive about watching my father work was where and how he began the picture. He would never start where you would expect, at least not where I would expect. When I would try to draw, I would always start with something simple and predictable, like the head.

I would build everything around that, often times, lopsided circle.
Not him though. My dad would start with the brow. I
mean seriously, he's drawing a picture of Spider-Man, and he
starts with the brow. Not the eyes mind you, and not even the
eyebrows, the brow. The section of your facial structure that's
kind of, but then not kind of, part of your skull. The part of your
face, that even though you don't realize it, portrays a
substantial portion of your face's emotional expressions. It's an
integral part of your non-verbal communication cues.
An inarguably vital key to your body language. But you would
never make that connection... unless you were an artist.

My dad made connections like that. He'd start a Spider-Man
picture at the brow and then work his way out from there. He'd
start at some place random and off-center and work his way out,
into a larger image, into a bigger picture. I would watch him
draw, peer over his shoulder and judge his work.

"That doesn't look like Spider-Man." I'd say at the tightly
curved lines of an in-discernible brow.

"Be patient, be patient..." He'd respond, bobbing his head
while still moving his pencil gracefully across the paper. His eyes
never leaving the task at hand. A man of focus. "It'll all come
together soon enough." he would assure me.

But I didn't see it. It didn't look like any Spider-Man I had
ever seen, didn't look like the image of Spider-Man that I had in
my head. What I didn't realize at the time, however, is that my
father also had an image in his head. He had his own image of
Spider-Man. He had a vision of his end goal. A starting point
from which to begin and a road map to get himself to his
intended destination. And it all started with a brow. I, on the
other hand, had only an inkling of an idea of what should be, and
in my youthful impatience, I jumped to a conclusion. I judged. I
doubted.

My dad is a good man, a great father and, as I have stressed, an excellent artist. So, of course, he was undeterred by my momentary lapse in faith. He just smiled and kept drawing. His hand never stopped moving. His eyes never left the page. His talent, instincts, and experience told him he was on the right track. And as a result, he was easily able to proceed with confidence, even though I was getting worried. As he continued his work and I continued to watch, more and more of the image would take form. Lines and shapes that seemed obscure at first would come into focus. Parts of the picture that were previously unclear would gradually become recognizable. Slowly begin to see the bigger picture. And as if watching a magician wave his hand and shout "Voilà!"... like magic, Spider-Man appeared.

I used to want to draw, I still do actually, and for a while I did. Never got as good as my old man though. Which is fine with me, to be honest, I don't think I ever really expected to become better than him at drawing. Still, my father taught me something by simply letting me watch him draw. And oddly, the things he taught me, are lessons that apply directly to my writing. He taught me to stay diligent, to focus on my vision and to see it through. He taught me that the picture is not always clear for the bystander or the onlooker, but as long as I can see the image in my head, then with patience, it'll come into focus for everyone else soon enough.

He taught me that most people will not understand your art in the midst of its creation. But as you get closer and closer to your end goal, the vision you've had all along, will become clear. And when they see it, their jaws will drop, their eyes will widen, and they will be in awe of the magic you made with your talent and your skill.

He taught me that the process is not for everyone else to understand, but as long as I understand, and as long as I keep working, as long as I keep my eyes on the page and my pencil on the paper, that everything will come together as it should. My father has taught me a ton of things in this life, but one lesson that I will always treasure is the time he taught me to be an artist.

*Note to self: I gotta get me a drafting table...

Like A Punch to the Face

It's an embarrassing thing to admit, but when I was younger, I used to get picked on.

Keep in mind that when I say "picked on" I don't mean I was being teased. No, it was more like I was getting beat up on a regular schedule. I was being bullied.

I know, I know... like I said, embarrassing. Unfortunately, it gets worse. The kid I was getting bullied by was this white boy, half my size. Not that his race should necessarily matter, but I want you to keep in mind that we were living in an all-black neighborhood at the time. So me, a black kid living in a black, respectably rough, neighborhood, getting seriously bullied by the smallest, whitest kid in a 3-mile radius was shameful to say the least.

I was 8 years old. Me and my mother were living in Litton Apartments in East Nashville. This kid Nathaniel lived on the same floor as me. My apartment was on one end of the hallway, and he lived on the other. We were practically neighbors, but this somehow had no positive effect on his extreme, seemingly unprovoked, dislike for me. Every time I saw Nathaniel outside of our hallway, there was violent conflict. One particular instance, a group of us neighborhood kids are standing around, simply talking, Nathaniel pops up without so much as a greeting to anyone in the group, he pushes me down, punches me at least twice in the face and stands over me, telling me to leave and go away. He's cursing and swearing, and I'm on the ground crawling backward like I'm trying to escape a monster in a horror movie. My eyes are welling up with tears, humiliated.

This was common practice for him and I, and for the life of me, I couldn't understand why. I was prepared to do anything to make it stop. I even tried being his friend. One day I invited him to my house to eat. Which for kids is a big deal to have someone outside your family eat with you, it's something usually reserved for best friends and potential play cousins. I remember it distinctly because my mother was making Hamburger Helper that night and it was Cheeseburger Macaroni, arguably the best flavored Hamburger Helper on the market. I ask my mom,

"Can my friend come eat with us?"

She reluctantly agrees, she doesn't know about the bullying, but she can sense something is not right. I go back to Nathaniel,

"Do you wanna come to my house and eat?" I sound like a straight up sucker.

Of course, he wants to come to my house and eat, he agrees with only a nod. So there he is sitting at my table eating my Cheeseburger Macaroni Hamburger Helper. Wolfing it down as if he had never eaten before, and my mother is sitting there with this look of disgust on her face. She still doesn't know the whole story, but I assume at the time, she knew enough. She knows we are not friends.

As you can imagine, my submissiveness and overall complete lack of dignity, did little to help the situation. Even after sitting in my house and eating my food Nathaniel was still giving me trouble. Still pushing me around and beating me up, and I was still taking it.

By nature, I am an introvert, quiet, soft-spoken and for the most part, a loner. This is especially true whenever I find myself in new surroundings, or in the presence of people I do not know. I tend to shy away from confrontation, and as I kid, I definitely had issues with confidence and self-esteem. Personality traits like these in an eight-year-old can tend to attract the attention of other kids who also have problems with self-esteem, confidence, and identity. It's a sad, yet logical, way of thinking that if you can just get at least one person to fall beneath you in the economic value system of self-worth, then you can always take comfort in the thought, "At least I'm not in last place." It is a foolish and superficial idea to take comfort in, but sometimes, when we are desperate, we are happy to settle with foolish and superficial ideas.

In the midst of this early life crisis, my cousin DJ comes over to the house to hang out for a couple of days. Now I have a lot of cousins, and we do this all the time. They come to my house and stay a couple of days, I go to their house and stay a couple of days, and we would just try to keep the cycle going for as long as possible. It's like our mothers did a kid exchange from time to time, but we all loved being together, so we encouraged the exchanges whenever the opportunity arose. I moved around a lot as a child, always in Nashville, but never in one neighborhood for too long. We moved from the west side to the east side, east side to the south side, and then from the south side back to the east side again. Rarely did I go to the same school two years in a row. It was always a new school, always new friends. But my cousins were a constant. They were my peer group and my comfort zone.

At a certain point during his stay DJ and I decided to walk to the store. Now to get to the store we have to walk up a small hill through half of the apartment complex and then cut through this small wooded area, literally like a small forest that sits right outside of Litton Apartments. We've made the trip a hundred times, it's a 15-minute walk there and back, it's nothing.

DJ and I step out of the makeshift forest on our return home from the store trip, we are laughing among ourselves, each of us with a large 2-liter bottle of soda cradled in our arms. We're still on the dirt trail when I see him. Nathaniel is standing there, directly in our path. He is with this other kid named Dontell. I know Dontell from the neighborhood, he was one of the more popular kids in Litton apartments. He had a slightly older brother that everyone kind of looked up to, and for some reason this made Dontell feel entitled to act like a bit of a jerk. Usually, whenever Nathaniel was giving me trouble, Dontell was not too far behind egging him on. Apparently, today was no different. Nathaniel stood there in silence, which was usually the case before an altercation between him and me broke out. He always stood around with these dead silent stares. I tried to play it cool.

"Watch out Nathaniel, I ain't even got time for you today," I say with a false air of confidence, as if all previous encounters had not been extraordinarily one-sided, as if every other time I'd seen him, my schedule had been open and clear for a degrading beat down. DJ is confused, me having a bully had never come up in general conversation, but he can sense the tension in the air, he stays quiet and simply follows suit. I try to step around Nathaniel, he takes a silent side step and blocks my path.

Damn... so here it is. Even with an ally along with me, Nathaniel is still undeterred. He is more than willing to embarrass me in front of my cousin, in fact, he's planning on it. This kid had been making my life hell for no earthly reason, and even now when he sees me smiling and laughing and happy and minding my own business, he's made it his duty to come rain on my parade.

The respect and admiration of my cousins was all I had left, it's all I ever really had as a kid. It was my primary source of identity and belonging. With my cousins, I wasn't shy and quiet and reserved. I was confident and smart and strong and brave. And now Nathaniel wanted to take that away from me too.

There was no fire in my belly. There was no split-second flashback of every time Nathaniel had ever punched, kicked, abused or embarrassed me, coming to my mind all at once. There was no rage. As a matter of fact, there was no emotion at all, not a single thought crossed my mind. I went to step around Nathaniel, he stepped out to block my path and POW!

It was like lightning struck. Without a single word and with one swift movement I dropped my soda and slammed my fist into Nathaniel's face. I punched him in the jaw so hard and so fast that neither he nor I even saw it coming. Everyone was quiet. Nathaniel stood there stunned and silent. He didn't move. After a second, I bent over and picked up my 2-liter soda bottle out of the dirt, and as I gathered it into my arms, I distinctly remember staring, for a moment at Nathaniel's shoes, they were so small... like a doll's feet. I stood up with my drink in hand and Nathaniel was still motionless. I walked pass him and began making my way home.

Dontell followed me and DJ as we walked down the hill through the apartment complex. He was poking and pushing me in the back trying to get a rise or response, trying to get me to turn around and face him, asking me who I thought I was and what did I think I was doing. But it was pointless, the gravity of what I had just done had started to set in, and I was beyond elated. I had crushed my bully with a single blow, and now I was a giant. In that moment, Dontell was about as significant to me, as a fly to an elephant. I was on cloud nine. I continued down the hill completely ignoring Dontell at my back. It wasn't long before I heard someone shout.

"DONTELL!!! LEAVE HIM ALONE!!!" Tony, Dontell's older brother, was standing in front of the building they lived in. He called Dontell away. I kept walking, DJ followed, he asked no questions.

We made it back to the house and went back to business as usual. I don't recall ever actually discussing our trip to the store at all. DJ never brought it up, and I never brought it up, at least not that I can remember. I do recall that later that same day DJ another cousin and I were in the hallway of my building, making up dance moves. Nathaniel's apartment door opened; he stepped out, jogged down to the end of the hallway where we were standing and without ever making eye contact, I mean with his eyes glued to the floor, he reached up and shook my hand. Then he turned around, jogged back down the hall and disappeared into his own apartment.

I didn't have any more issues with Nathaniel after that day.

Gunsmoke

I used to be convinced that I would die young.

And by that I mean, there was a certain time, I think around the age of 11 or 12, that I was pretty sure I would not live past the age of 23. I don't know what it was that gave me that idea. Perhaps it was during a time when I was watching a lot of movies about being young and black and growing up in the inner city, and in all those movies, the good kids died at a young age and usually at the hands of violence. Not to mention the news, seemed like I was always hearing a story of the guy with the promising future being killed in some tragic incident. Being somewhere at the wrong place at the wrong time, and now sadly gone too soon.

For so long I was convinced that's how my story would end. Nathan McDougal, wrong place, wrong time, gone too soon.

Eventually, I outgrew such thoughts. But, it's not really the thoughts you have to outgrow.

When I was 15, I almost joined a gang. Almost. Delvin and I were hanging out a lot with my older cousin Gene back then. Now, Delvin was my best friend and had been since about the age of 6. And Gene, well Gene was not actually my cousin at all, but rather, he was the best friend of my cousin Michael. Here is the thing: In my community, and by "my community" I mean, the inner city, poverty-stricken, African American community particularly of the Southern United States, friends don't just stay friends. Once we have known someone for an extended amount of time, especially when those relationships originate in childhood, friends graduate into family and "my friend" simply becomes, "my cousin." Gene had been best friends with my cousin Michael since before I could even think to say, they were like brothers, and so by default, Gene was, for all intents and purposes, my cousin.

Me and Delvin were hanging with Gene and Gene was a part of a gang. A very small, very local gang from Nashville's west side. They wore red bandannas, when bandannas were called for, were all fiercely loyal to one another and could be rather wild from time to time. Gene was silly, fun-loving and kind-hearted, and as a result, the gang was very similar; a good group of guys that just so happen to be a roving band of teenage criminals. Call it what you will, but for us, it was life.

So one day Delvin and I were with the gang, and someone yells out.

"Man, Nate, and Delvin be around so much we might as well gon put them down."

"Put them down" means to initiate into the gang usually by being beaten to the satisfaction of, as well as, by, already existing members of the gang. Being initiated into a gang this way is supposed to be a display of the possible recruit's strength, ferocity, and determination as it was expected of you to fight back against overwhelming odds, and to stand your ground even in the face of imminent defeat.

When this statement was made, the only thing that followed was silence. Delvin and I kind of stare at one another with an, "Oh Shit!" kind of expression stamped across our faces, which then quickly faded into a shoulder-shrugging "I guess we're joining a gang" kind of expression. The idea of being in a gang was not far-fetched for either of us. In some ways, it was inevitable.

But before either Delvin or I could respond, Gene interjects, "Man, hell naw!" he says with a big grin "Nate take karate, he'll beat everybody ass if we try and jump him in!" Gene erupts in laughter, the whole gang erupts in laughter, the topic of Delvin and I joining the gang never comes up again. Crisis averted.

Gene knew my father, which meant he knew of my father's absolute zero tolerance policy for gang activity, suspected, implied or inferred. He also knew that my father had put me in karate classes in an attempt to streamline my hand-eye coordination for football. He was looking out for me, he saw me in a tight spot so he stepped in; he intervened. He kept me out of the gang, without kicking me out of the gang. That's the type of guy he was, a good guy, through and through.

Gene and I grew up together, so even outside the gang, we hung out a lot. He had taken me under his wing and even more than a "cousin" he treated me like a little brother.

One day he and I were riding in his mom's car. It was me, him, Rod, who was from the gang, Amanda, Gene's younger sister, and Amanda's friend, whose name I can't remember. The car is only a two-door sedan, and there are five of us inside. Gene is driving, Rod is navigating, and I'm squeezed into the backseat with the two girls.

We are heading to a young woman's house. Someone Rod knows, she has a friend that she wants to introduce to Gene.

We pull up to this girl's house in a neighborhood called Trinity Hills. Sitting on her porch are about five guys, apparently from the neighborhood. We park in the driveway. Rod and Gene hop out, me and the girls are still in the back. This is supposed to be a quick pit stop, no need for everyone to get out of the car.

"Where ya homegirl at?" Rod asked, ignoring the large group of random guys sitting in the shadow of her front door.

"She's on her way up here now," she responded, also pretending the group of guys on her porch are some type of collective hallucination.

Gene is standing outside of the car by the driver side door. He's tall, 6'3 maybe 6'4. He looks skinny, but he's not. He's lean. A natural born athlete. For a period of time we were both on the high school track team. He ran the longer races, like the mile, the half-mile; he made them look easy. When everyone else was dead tired and dragging across the track like they were about to pass out, he was making funny faces at the crowd. Before that, we were on the swim team for the Hadley Park community center. He swam like a fish.

Both Gene and Rod are talking to Rod's young lady friend. Gene is wearing a navy blue Nike t-shirt, on the front is a fork and on the back is the phrase "Eat Dirt." The windows to the car are down, and I can hear the guys on the porch begin to snicker and giggle.

"This nigga got a fork on his shirt." They whisper to themselves and then begin laughing.

Gene looks up from his conversation.

"Aye! What you say?" Gene speaks toward the porch.

The group of boys began to bumble.

"Who he talking to?" One of them ask.

"Nigga he talking to you!" Another one of them responds.

"Aw shit," Says another one of the boys and he immediately hops out of a chair and walks into the house. He mumbles something about calling someone, but he trails off as the door closes behind him.

"What he say bruh?" Rod asked Gene, but Gene is not paying attention.

"You know what?" Gene says, still speaking to the porch. "I'll be right back, and none of ya'll better be here when I get back." Gene hops back into the car and slams the door. Rod hops back into the passenger seat. "They got me fucked up," Gene says, he's still smiling. It's like he's happy, even when he's angry.

We drive back to the west side, back to the Preston Taylor Housing Projects. The gang's base of operations. Gene drops off Amanda, and her friend, while he, Rod and I ride through the neighborhood on a new mission. See, there was the gang, but things did not all begin and end with the gang. In reality, the whole neighborhood was a loosely affiliated gang, and by simply being from the west side put the entire neighborhood at your disposal in times of need. We were on The Drive, a very specific subsection of our public housing project, when Gene pulls up on Junnie.

Junnie is in the gang, he and Gene are best friends, nearly inseparable. He explains what happens in Trinity Hills, and immediately Junnie is on board. The only logical response that any of them have from our interaction in Trinity Hills is to go back and beat the ass of every guy standing outside that house. Gene tells Junnie, and Junnie tells Bert, Bert agrees to join us too. Bert is not in the gang, but he is a respected west sider. He's like a

West Nashville Patriot, completely down for the cause. He is sitting in a car with a girl that doesn't live in the projects but goes to our school, and even she is down to ride back to Trinity Hills with us. It's her car that they're sitting in, and before anyone can even ask, she volunteers to drive.

There are a few more people with us as well. I can't remember who all else was there, but before we head out, we form a makeshift game plan. There is a gun. Only one, I can't even recall exactly where it came from. It may have been one of those weapons that belonged to someone from the crew that kind of floated from person to person. Either way, we had it, and we only had one. The plan was simple. Pull up to the house, jump out and beat up everyone outside. But most importantly, do not pull out the gun unless it's absolutely necessary. Very simple, pull up, jump out, beat up everybody, don't pull out the gun unless we need it. Easy. The perfect plan. It couldn't possibly go wrong.

We leave Preston Taylor in three cars. Rap music blaring from the speakers of the small two-door sedan. We're speeding, zipping in and out of traffic, racing one another as we zoom through the streets. Our cars are rocking. Excitement and adrenaline have overthrown logic and reason, and the only thing left is the mission. I'm in the back seat again, I'm the youngest of the gang, so it's only natural. But while everyone is getting hyped up about the task at hand, I couldn't help but sit back and think how all this was a horrible and unequivocally bad idea.

At this particular moment, our radio is playing Juvenile. It's the title track from his "400 Degreez" album. Junnie's car speeds up beside ours, Rod is now in the car with Junnie. He leans forward from the passenger seat bouncing up and down with pre-fight energy. He has the gun in his hands, and he is rapping along to whatever song they are listening to as if he is filming a music video. I shake my head in disapproval, "Do not pull out the gun unless we need it." It was a simple rule, and he's already broken it. I protest.

"What is he doing? Put the gun down nigga!" I scream across the speeding cars. I turn to Gene. "He tripping."

"Hell yeah, they bullshitting." Gene agrees, a broad smile plastered across his face.

He's laughing, as both Junnie and Rod are rapping out the lyrics of their song word for word. The cars are swerving away from one another and then quickly jumping back to parallel lanes. In our car Juvenile is still rapping. I pause, taking in the entire scene and for a moment times slows to a crawl. Energy begins to transfer. Juvenile's lyrics are echoing through my head and it's almost like we are in a scene from a John Singelton movie. My old visions of dying young... well, they had been gone for some time by now, and all that I am left with is the moment. The music from 400 Degreez is reverberating throughout the interior of the car and the vibrations penetrate my very being. I look at Junnie and Rod across traffic, their faces are twisted and turned up into tough frowns, but the frowns never last long before the smiles squeeze through again. I look at Gene, and he's laughing, and a gleeful grin stretches from one ear to the other. My doubts about our decisions begin to fade. Juvenile is rapping. His voice is surprisingly loud, crisp and clear amid the chaos of rushing wind and speeding traffic.

"How I'm gon be running with these killers and backing down; how I'm gon look in front of my people; like a clown?"

Juvie's words ring throughout my inner mind, echoing and replaying themselves in an infinite loop. It's like I'm just now hearing the song for the first time and now it finally makes sense. The gang is ecstatic at the thought of conflict, there is no doubt, no anxiety, they are either mentally prepared for all possible outcomes, or they simply do not care.

Yeah, *"How am 'I' going to be running with these killers, and backing down?"* For the past year and a half, the gang had fully embraced me, taken me in as one of their own, without question. They were like family. Gene *was* family. Who was I to back out on them now, to back out on Gene? *"How am I going to look in front of my people...like a clown?"* And suddenly my anxiety dissipated. Energy transfer complete. "Fuck it," I say to myself, and I too began bouncing to the music.

We pull all three cars into the front yard of the girl's house to find the boys still sitting outside. I see one boy immediately retreat into the house at the sight of us.

"I told you I'd be back didn't I!" Gene jumps out of the car and immediately dashes into the yard with his shirt off.

The damn car is a two-door, so I have to reach up and move the seat to let myself out. In doing this, my eyes break from the scene in the yard for a brief moment. Once I make my way out of the car, I look back to the yard to see that the chaos and energy from the drive over has spilled out into the girl's driveway. Gene is in front of the house. He takes two skips forward, leans in and swings with his right, the punch is reckless and wild, he's trying to knock out the kid who made the fork comment. The jokester dodges, but only barely. He's backpedaling trying to keep his distance from Gene as best he can, but it's difficult. Gene is tall and fast and breathing down the kid's neck, giving him little to no room to operate. On the other side of the yard, Rod has jumped out of Junnie's car and is jumping up and down, flailing the gun in the air and screaming at the same time.

"Yea nigga, what's up with all that shit now!" Rod yells out, but the only one to respond is Rod's female friend. She is also jumping up and down and screaming, only in her hand, there is only a cordless telephone.

"Rod stop! Why are you doing this?!" She heaves the phone in his direction, and it shatters against the pavement. Rod is unaffected, he continues flailing the gun. None of the guys from the porch seem to be interested in having a conversation with Rod, they are either running or ducking or fighting one of my friends. I shake my head. We had one rule.

I look over to my right at one of the other cars that came with us and see I am not the only one who is not in the yard, actively engaged in combat. Bert is standing back leaning on the front hood of his car watching everything unfold. He looks over to me.

"These fools crazy," he says with a smile and a chuckle.

"Man, yeah they are." I agree as I too lean up against the trunk of Gene's car.

We have pulled up into someone else's neighborhood with guns and gangsters. All with the intentions of doing someone bodily harm. And it is to laugh.

Internally, I breathe a sigh of relief. We've won the day, we have the muscle, and the manpower and the situation is entirely under our control. I know now that no one will be seriously hurt, after all, we really only came to scare. To possibly black an eye and bruise an ego. To instill fear, not to kill. For this, I am relieved.

And then power changes hands.

The tires of the two vehicles let off a high-pitched screech as the cars slam to a stop, the doors fly open, and everyone who hops out has a gun in his hand.

"Nuh-unh' don't run now!" One of them calls out.

My reaction time is slow, I turn around to see them standing across a small two-lane street. Maybe about 20 feet from me. Guns drawn. All pointed in my direction.

I watch one of the guns go off. There is a small flame that leaps from the barrel, hardly even visible in the daylight, a puff of white translucent smoke dissipates almost as quickly as it appears and there is a loud auditory pop. The gun I'm staring down goes off at least twice before I realize I'm staring death in the face, and I snap out of it. I break to my left in an attempt to get out of the line of fire. Gene's car is in the opposite direction but so are the other guys with guns, so I am forced to make do with what I have. Against my better judgment, I turn my back on the people shooting at us and rip open the back door to the car Bert came in, and I dive inside. The car is already full, and I am practically on top of someone. I don't even have enough room to close the door behind me. And the only thing going through my head is how I'm about to get shot in the back and spend the rest of my life in a wheelchair. Just my luck.

The girl that volunteered to drive over with us speeds away. The word of the day had been "Chaos," and the theme continued over into our getaway. As we raced down the street, it was realized that not everyone had made it into a car. I see Junnie and Rod running down the street, completely shirtless with big broad smiles on their faces. We were all just standing in front of a firing squad, and they are laughing like we just left a comedy club. Rod screams out something indistinguishable and points our one gun into the air and pulls the trigger, letting off two shots in quick succession before hopping into Junnie's car. The car I'm in speeds down a hill around a corner and then makes a few more twists and turns. We end up coming down a hill that dumps us out on to Clarksville Pike, a major street north of the city. The frenzy in the car continues. Turns out Bert did not hop into the car that he arrived in, the car that I am currently in, and we don't know if he is in one of the other cars. As we come up to Clarksville Pike, the girl in the car is telling me to get out of her car and get in the car with Gene.

"Where are they?" I ask.

"They're right over there, you'll see them as soon as you get out, straight ahead."

I hop out of the car in the middle of traffic, and I don't see anybody. I think I hear someone calling out to me but there are cars everywhere and I can't tell who is who. As a result, I do the only logical thing I can think of. I run out of the street to the nearby sidewalk and begin casually strolling down Clarksville Pike as if I were not just involved in a shootout.

I am horrible with directions, but fortunately for me, the area we were in was somewhat familiar. After a quick look around I knew that Tennessee State University was nearby, and just so happens Preston Taylor Public Housing sits right next to Tennessee State. I make my way to a storefront and grab hold to a pay phone. I consider making a collect call, but I can't decide who I would make the call too, so I just put the phone down. I see a guy coming out of the store.

"Excuse me, which direction is TSU?" I ask.

He points me south, and I start walking.

It's summertime, the sun is out, and I can actually see the university in the distance. It's going to be a long walk, but it's manageable. I convince myself that not jumping in the other car was the smartest thing to do. There must have been at least 15 shots fired in a residential neighborhood, and the last place I needed to be was in a speeding car with a loaded gun. Yeah, now I was making well thought out choices. After the fact.

"Nate! Nathan!" I hear someone calling my name. It's Gene. He's in the backseat of a completely different car, and a completely different girl is driving. He waves me over, "Come on get in!"

I dash over to the car and hop into the back seat. Gene is explaining to the woman driving what happened and how we ended up in our current predicament. She was Gene's age, probably around 18 or 19. I recognized her from the neighborhood, but for the life of me, I couldn't tell you her name at this point in time. The girl was mad, when Gene was not explaining himself she was scolding him and the rest of us for making such stupid decisions. He offered no argument. He simply agreed with her every point and apologized whenever he wasn't agreeing.

Apparently, I wasn't the only one missing in action. Turns out Bert had not been in any of the other cars either. Gene had made it back to Preston Taylor, saw that neither Bert nor I were accounted for and had come back out to find us. I was rather easy to find as I imagine someone told him I had hopped out of the car on Clarksville Pike and that was all he needed to track me down. Bert, on the other hand, had not been seen since the shooting started.

In order to find Bert, we had no choice but to ride back through Trinity Hills, back to where the shooting took place. The girl driving told me and Gene to duck down in the back seat of the car so we wouldn't be seen. We drove back past Rod's friend's house. Both me and Gene in the back of the car attempting to make ourselves as small as possible, scrunched down into contorted positions trying our best to be invisible. We made a pass through the neighborhood but came up empty-handed. Bert was nowhere to be found. Gene and I were dropped back off in the projects once again as the girl was going to go back out and make another pass through to try and find Bert. We arrived back at Gene's house on The Drive, his mother was sitting on the porch smoking a cigarette. She had been filled in on at least some version of what had happened and she was livid. There was more scolding, and I remember feeling both ashamed and embarrassed at the blatantly bad decision we had made, yet somehow, even in retrospect, it had seemed so desperately unavoidable that I cannot imagine that afternoon having played out in any other way than how it did. And while I can point out multiple instances in which the series of events could have been derailed, and an alternate ending attained. The personalities and interplay of the gang combined with the fragile and volatile whims of the young male ego locked us into a set of chain reactions that were as inevitable and irreversible as a sunset.

I can't remember if it was Cassandra, Gene's mother, who told me to go call my dad or if I did it of my own volition. I just remember making the call.

If staring down the barrel of a gun had not been terrifying enough, calling Big Reggie to tell him you had been staring down the barrel a gun was. I was inside Gene's house when I made the call. He picked up after the second ring.

"Daddy,"

"What's up?"

"Man umm, I was with Gene and Rod, and we went to this girl house and got to arguing with some dudes in the neighborhood got into a fight and um... they ended up shooting at us."

".... I'm on my way to get you."

"Ok."

Click. Conversation ended. I had conveniently left out how we had left the neighborhood, went back to the projects gathered up a posse, then went back to the neighborhood with a gun in our own possession, hopped out of three cars, tried to beat up everyone in the neighborhood, then got ambushed by the residents of said neighborhood.

The day had been intense, my adrenaline was spilling over, and I'm sure there was some trembling in my voice as I spoke. My father probably thought I was traumatized by the ordeal. He didn't ask for any details or additional explanation, nor did I offer any. He was just "on his way." That worked for me. I would rather have gone back and taken my chances in Trinity Hills than have an angry Reggie Wade on his way to pick me up.

I went back out to the porch where Gene and the other guys were standing. Cassandra was still upset, and she was letting us know exactly how much. Not that I could blame her. Gene just kept trying to explain himself, but she would hear none of it. I remember this next moment quite distinctly. We were on the porch, and Cassandra was smoking a cigarette, I was sitting on the metal railing not more than a few feet from her. And at that moment my body was so amped up on adrenaline that when I inhaled the second-hand smoke from her cigarette, I could feel the leftover nicotine hit my nervous system and begin to try and ease my tension. I hadn't realized until that moment how mentally wrecked I was. Not until that second-hand cigarette smoke started to go to work on my frazzled nerve endings.

Before too long, they found Bert. He was okay. In all the confusion he just bolted in some random direction altogether, as opposed to jumping into a car. He had a few bumps and bruises but overall was no worse for the wear. I saw him later that same day as he rode off in the car with one of his family members.

"Aight man, I'll holla at ya'll later," he said as he leaned on the door poking his head out of the window.

I was relieved that nothing had happened to him. In the end, everyone made it out of the ordeal okay. Cassandra's car had few bullet holes in it, a couple by the driver's side door and another near the gas tank.

My dad got to Gene's house right as the sun begin to set. I hopped in the car, and we headed home. He didn't ask for too many more details about the ordeal, and I didn't volunteer any. There was nothing else that needed to be said.

Gene and his mom and his sister eventually moved out of Preston Taylor to an apartment in Bellevue, a neighborhood further west of the city. This was maybe a year later. Gene's house had been a central meeting place for the gang, and while his moving didn't break up the crew, it weakened *my* ability to hang out as much. A year or two after that I graduated from high school, and I went off to college. The gang kept being the gang, and I stayed in touch when I could.

Some ten years later, in January 2010 my cousin Gene was shot and killed outside of Nashville, Tennessee. He was 29 years old.

When I was a kid, I use to be convinced that I would die young because they say "The Good Die Young," But as I got older, I realized, it's not the good that are taken at a young age... it's the best that are taken at a young age.

Rest in Peace to my brother, Stanley Eugene Gregory Jr.

A great man gone too soon.

Go Kinfolk, Go Kinfolk

When I started driving, whenever I would leave the house, particularly with a group of friends, my mother would yell out, before I could even get out of the door, "Seatbelts, Speed limit." This was a reminder for us to wear our seatbelts and drive the speed limit. She still says that to me to this day, and me being me, I still don't listen.

Delvin and I have been friends for a long time. Seems like, since the beginning of time. We go back, way back, almost further then I can remember.

We used to play football together at this community center in South Nashville called Rose Park. We played there for all of six years, and the field was like a home away from home for us. I remember one day in particular. We were about ten years old, and our team that year was called the Mary Pruitt Saints. See our team changed names every couple of years, whenever we got a new sponsor, and this year we were the saints. It was a Saturday, we had just finished a game, and the fields were soaking wet because it had rained heavily that morning as well as the day before. All over the park, there were these large puddles of rainwater. I mean huge puddles that looked like small ponds dotting the landscape of the park.

Delvin and I were coming off the field. We had already taken off
our shoulder pads and our helmets and were in full out mischief
mode. We came up to one of those gigantic rainwater puddles, and
I can't recall who suggested it first, but I have to assume it was
Delvin who said to me.

"I bet you won't dive into that water?"

And I respond with a simple, "I'll do it if you do it."

We drop our equipment and take a few steps back. A running
start is only fitting for a challenge like this. At the count of three, we
both break into a sprint, running towards the pool of open water.
Legs are kicking, arms are pumping, and we are moving fast as we
hit the edge of the water. It's ankle... no, shin deep, but that's as far
as it goes, we splash through, still running, neither of us diving in.
We don't trust each other. The entire time we were running, I'm
looking at Delvin, he's looking at me, and we are trying to figure
out who is going to back out first. Who is trying to make the other
look like a dummy for diving face first into a giant puddle of dirty
rainwater?

"You didn't do it!"

"You didn't do it!"

"That's because I knew you were gonna back out!"

"No, I knew you were gonna back out!"

"Fine let's go again, and this time we'll do it for real." We agree.
We go back to our starting point and before we begin to count
down an idea strikes. I reach over to Delvin and grab hold to his
shirt, forming a vice-like grip on his back collar, and without words,
he reaches over and also gets a tight grip onto mine.

We break into another sprint, each with a fist full of the other's t-shirt. Mutually assured destruction. We hit the edge of the water again, but this time, we don't run through. One, two steps into the puddle and I go for it. I commit, and in an instant I'm airborne. I glide through the air, and for a moment I seem to just hang there, wholly immune to the laws of physics or any and all of the effects of gravity. I go into a descent; my chest hitting the surface of the water before anything else and like a thrown stone I'm skidding across puddle with a surprising amount of momentum. Water is sliding up on either side of me, and I feel like a human boogie board. You ever drive your car through a large puddle and watch the water flare up on the left and the right. At that moment I was the front bumper. I must have been running faster than I thought because I kept sliding forward further then what seemed logically possible, and then before I knew it, I stopped. We stopped.

I looked over and saw Delvin had just taken the same ride as I. We stood up, soaked to the bone and covered from head to toe in dead grass. My uncle Troy was there, he coached at Rose Park along with my father. He came across the two of us, dripping water and spitting grass out of our mouths.

"Why are ya'll so wet?" he asked in bewilderment.

"We dove through that puddle over there." One of us answered.

I don't think he ever even asked why. He took us to his truck, gave us new shirts to put on, and sent us back on our way.

After we exceeded the Rose Park age limit of 12, we never played football together again, but still managed to stay close friends. So close in fact, that we didn't refer to each other as friends anymore, just cousins. During the summer we would stay at one another's house for weeks on end. It got to the point to where my father would have to force me to come home, and force Delvin to stay home.

By 15 or 16 both Delvin and I had earned quite a bit of autonomy, and for the most part, we were left to do as we pleased, granted, we stayed out of trouble. We were right on the cusp of driving age and on the edge of what we knew would be true freedom. Anytime either one of us could get our hands on some car keys we did. One would go pick up the other, and we would spend our days and nights exploring the city from the driver and passenger seat of a car. Driving through downtown Nashville, going to movies and going to the mall, finding parties and hangouts and always searching for the ever-popular Teen Night.

In Nashville, Teen Night, was when clubs and often times hotel ballrooms, would rent out space to a party promoter who would then throw parties and events for kids ages 17 and under. Sounds innocent enough. It wasn't. These Teen Nights were testosterone charged battlegrounds where numerous fights, shootings and other random acts of wanton violence took place. At one such event, I remember standing outside of a venue, waiting in line to get in, and I overhear a police officer sigh and say to another officer nearby. "Man, I'd rather work riot squad then do teen night."

That's how vicious these teenage parties used to be. If the average Metropolitan Police officer was given a choice between a riot line and a large group of unruly, bloodthirsty, sex-crazed teenagers, they'd choose the riot.

Meanwhile, we were breaking our necks to attend Teen Night at every available opportunity. Needless to say, whenever we could get our hands on a car, this is where we went.

Teen Night consisted primarily of two phases. Inside the venue, where you did one of two things. Try and get a girl to dance with you, and by "dance" with you I mean to have a girl grind her butt vivaciously against your pelvis. This was called "getting twerked on." Before twerking was mainstream it was the number one reason a young man would venture into the jaws of death known as Teen Night. You would risk life and limb for a chance to get twerked on. Either that or you were picking a fight. When the girls weren't dancing, or even sometimes when they were, the center of the dance floor would turn into a makeshift mosh pit. Groups of guys from different parts of town would try and establish their dominance by pushing, shoving, elbowing and eventually by flat out punching one another, all perfectly in-synch to the overdeveloped bass of everyone's favorite hip-hop songs.

That was phase one, inside the venue. Phase two took place outside the venue, in the parking lot. Once again with two options, the first being picking up where you left off inside the party. Fights started inside would spill out to the street, as well as conversations and relationships started under the hypnosis of gyrating hips. If you could land the name and phone number of a cute girl that you danced with inside the party, it was a good night. If you could do so without someone stomping on your head anywhere in the process, it was a great night.

The second part of phase two took place once you made it to your car. In part two of phase two, all of the teenagers run out to the parking lot, jump into their cars and leave.

Only thing is, exiting the parking lot is an ordeal that takes anywhere for thirty to forty-five minutes, mainly because each teenager takes roughly 3 to 4 laps around the parking lot itself, driving erratically and recklessly the entire time. We use to call this "yanking it" or sometimes referred to it as "swerving." The key was to take wide, dangerous, what my father used to call "Cadillac turns." If you are turning left, then you'd accelerate gently and turn the wheel to the right, and at the absolute last moment you press the gas down hard and yank the steering wheel left. The car's engine would rev, and the vehicle would rise up and bound forward swinging and pitching under the stress of the spontaneous direction change. Then, before you hit someone or something, you slam on the brakes, change direction and accelerate again. Sometimes you weren't even doing a full turn, we'd actually do this within a single car lane, all in the venue parking lot.

This is where Delvin excelled. For the most part, I had always imagined Delvin, and I were on equal footing in pretty much everything we did. Where he was faster, I was stronger. Whenever my size played to my advantage, his agility played to his. We were always different but still always evenly matched. When it came to driving, however, I was completely and utterly outclassed. Delvin would drive like a maniac, but still, always maintain complete control of the vehicle. His reaction time and reflexes were inhuman, and whenever he was behind the wheel of a car, it was an amazing thing to behold.

Now flash forward some eight to nine years after the puddle jumping episode. It's summertime. Delvin and I are about 16 years old, and we are hanging out at his house on South Fourth Street in East Nashville. By this time in our lives Delvin had begun hustling, and by that, I mean he had begun his budding career as a street-level drug dealer. He'd sell crack to old fiends in and around South Fourth Street. I'd be with him as he would do hand-to-hand transactions with these old men who would try and cheat him and teach him at the same time.

"Come on D, you gotta give me a lil more than that baby boy," they loved to complain about the size of the rock they received for the $10 or $20 he was charging them. "You know I'm gon spend with you all weekend. Let me win this time, and I'll let you win next time." Their negotiation skills were to be applauded, and usually, Delvin gave in to their request, within reason.

Delvin used to actually make his sales just to scrape up enough money for us to pay our way into Teen Night. Neither of us had a car of our own at the time, so in order for us to go anywhere without a chaperone one of us had to borrow a car, usually either from father, Big Reggie or from Delvin's mother, Sweet.

This particular night, for reasons I can't remember we were desperate to get out of the house, off of South Fourth and into the city. Delvin asked Sweet if we could borrow her car to go to a Teen Night at a nearby venue called the Stadium Inn, a shady rundown hotel that was notorious for its violent Teen Night parties. We were chomping at the bit to get there but had Sweet denied Delvin's request to borrow the car and wouldn't budge on her position. Delvin fumed. He was angrier then what seems reasonable but that's Delvin for you, he's always a short fuse. He stormed out of the house, still trying to figure out a way for us to get to Stadium Inn. I followed him outside. The night air was warm. We strolled around the neighborhood listlessly for a while, and slowly Delvin's determination began to fade. A couple of hours passed, and it seemed assured that we weren't going anywhere for the night.

The social circle of a young drug dealer is far more expansive than that of your average 16-year-old. There is a network of resources made available to you, that simply are not accessible to standard civilians. On top of that, being a hustler offers a young person from neighborhoods like ours a small amount of celebrity status usually only afforded to star athletes. Coincidentally, Delvin was both, so right when our evening should have been clearly marked as a loss, suddenly it was not.

As Delvin and I were standing outside, his anger from our lack of mobility finally regressing. A car pulls up, stops right in front of us and out hops this guy I recognize as VJ. He and Delvin are friends.

"What up Del?" VJ says as he exits the vehicle, he doesn't even bother putting it into a parking space or cutting off the ignition. He just hops out.

"What up VJ," Delvin responds "Got a new whip didn't ya?"

"Man, I probably had this for a couple weeks now."

The car was a caprice, highly sought after during that time, it was obviously a few years old, maybe a 95' not old enough to be a classic and not new enough to truly impress. It was an odd bluish green color, long and round. I personally preferred the older model Caprice, the ones that had the distinct edges and corners, more in the box style. But then again, I was car-less, so I really couldn't afford to be too picky. Any car was better than no car, and this wasn't just any car, it was a good find. Any kid our age would be happy to have it, new paint job, an incredibly loud sound system and a set of oversized rims and you'd skyrocket up the social strata. Drug Dealers, Athletes, and Guys with Cool Cars, instantly you'd be ranked among the best of the best.

"Shid let me drive," Delvin asked without hesitation.

"Gon head," VJ responded.

I was confused. What was happening? Where did VJ come from and why was he so willingly parting ways with a new car. Delvin wasn't bogged down with such questions. Before VJ could even fully finish saying yes, Delvin had dashed over to Sweet's car, opened the door, grab something out of the center console and was behind the wheel of VJ's car, all in an instant.

"Come on Nate!" he yelled out, one foot in the vehicle and one hand on the steering wheel. I went to jump into the backseat and Delvin waved me around to the front passenger seat.

"Is VJ not coming with us?" I asked.

"Hell na'll," Delvin said with a grin, "This mafucka ours for the night."

Delvin hit the gas and sped away from South Fourth Street leaving VJ standing on the sidewalk alone and without protest. He began to fumble around with the radio at which point I saw what he had grabbed from Sweet's car before we left. It was a CD.

At this time in our lives, Delvin and I were both big Nas fans. I had discovered his music during my freshman year in high school, and I brought my findings over to Delvin. We latched on to the style and swagger of the Queen's Bridge Rapper with unabashed enthusiasm, we were walking around in forward-facing Eddie Bauer Dad hats before it was socially acceptable all because we had seen Nas do it first.

Delvin pushed in the CD and skipped down to an already predetermined song.

"We about to hit up Teen Night," he said as he hit the play button. A woman's voice cut into the car, crisp and clear.

"Oh yeah Mafucka, that's that shit!" her voice was rugged and gruff, and she had heavy New York accent. Nas came in immediately after her.

"Ladies make it hot, thugs make it hot, make it pop." When Nas says "pop" the beat comes in loud and heavy, and then, the chorus starts. I knew this song, it was a favorite of mine for all of the wrong reasons.

"Oo-chie wally wally, oo-chie bang bang

Oo-chie wally wally, oo-chie bang bang

Oo-chie wally wally, oo-chie bang bang" The chorus is sung by a woman, who may or may not have been the same woman from the song's introduction.

Oochie Wally is a sexually explicit song that celebrates all forms of debauchery and depravity. Needless to say, I loved it. And as quiet as its kept, just between you and me, I still love it. It's a great song.

It only took a few minutes to get to Stadium Inn. As we are entering the parking lot, we can see that Teen Night is ending. The kids are leaving the venue and spilling out into the parking lot heading to their cars. It was the start of the second phase. By now the CD was playing some other random song as we drove into the far end of a parking lot that had to be roughly 150 yards in length. With a grin, Delvin reached down to the CD player and changed the song back to Oochie Wally, hit the "repeat" button, turned up the volume as high as it would go, and pushed down hard on the gas pedal. The engine revved and the car lurched forward, not that you could really hear the engine over the sound system. The car stereo radiated "Oochie Wally" in every direction.

"Oo-chie wally wally, Oo-chie bang bang,"

The people leaving out of the party could both hear us and see us coming. Delvin was swerving; yanking the car from side to side. The music was blaring, the engine was roaring, and I can swear through the chaos I heard at least one person say, "Hey it's Delvin." and as if a celebrity had arrived, the crowd started going crazy.

Delvin lived only a few miles from Stadium Inn, went to high school nearby and was well known in the area, as hustlers and athletes usually are. But our arrival seemed to mark a new level of excitement. People begin swarming the car, but Delvin didn't slow down. We kept swerving back and forth, speeding up and then braking hard, causing the car to rev and screech in quick succession. The entire time Nas and company are still loudly spouting in rhyme, infeasible sexual exploits that would make a sailor blush.

Soon we were surrounded by teenagers, everyone trying to get Delvin to stop for a moment. He wouldn't. He just kept driving, and the parking lot quickly turned into a rap music video. Guys started jumping onto the car. They would jump up and sit on the hood, pumping their arms up and down in sync with the music, and at the same time shouting "Aye, Aye, Aye, Aye!" as if it were some ancient African ritual war chant, they ones that were known to put you in a trance or send you into a frenzy. Everyone seemed both empowered and encouraged by it, Delvin from behind the wheel, the mob of kids surrounding the car, and the select few guys who were hitching a ride on the hood of our rampaging caprice. And yet, not even this, changed the way Delvin drove. Yanking, swerving. He would speed forward, turn the wheel sharply to the right or the left, then stop abruptly. The wheels would screech to a halt, and the frame of the car would lurch forward from the momentum and the guys on the hood of the car would slide off and land gently on their feet. Delvin was not doing this intentionally, and yet it seemed so extremely well-coordinated that you would have thought it was choreographed.

"Oo-chie wally wally, Oo-chie bang bang."

The girls in the parking lot reacted as well. They started dancing. Twerking. Hands on knees, booty shaking and hips gyrating. Right there in the parking lot, amidst a barreling and careening vehicle controlled by someone barely old enough to drive, all in synch to Oochie Wally.

The guys are jumping on to the hood of the car, girls are twerking in the street, and Delvin is swerving in and out this sea of people like he's taking some type of post-apocalyptic driving course. Another guy slides off the hood of the car, Delvin speeds forward another measly ten feet, as there are too many people to go any further any faster. There is a girl in front of us, I don't even see her until the absolute last minute, but I imagine she has see us and hears us well in advance. She makes no effort to move out of the way of the speeding vehicle, and as if the car is not even there, she turns her back to us and starts dancing like everyone else. We are going fast, and she is too close to swerve around. I place one hand on the dashboard brace myself and yell "Yo-yo-yo-yo!"

Delvin slams on the brakes and the car screeches as the rubber wheels slide violently across the asphalt with a loud "skrrrrrt," before stopping a few feet short of the dancing girl. The girl doesn't flinch, doesn't scream, doesn't run out of the way, she just keep dancing. It's almost like she's in a trance. The whole crowd is in a frenzy.

"Oo-chie wally wally, Oo-chie bang bang."

Delvin turns the wheel sharply to the right, accelerates and zooms off around her. We barrel out of the Stadium Inn parking lot, Occhie Wally still playing, the crowd in our rearview, still going wild.

A couple of years pass, and by now Delvin and I are nearly seniors in high school. It is another summer night. We are in Sweet's car, which is an early 90's Oldsmobile. We called it the Blue Chew, for no reason other than, the car was blue.

This particular night Teen Night was not at Stadium Inn. It was at another hotel, this one on Trinity Lane, not as close, but still not too far away, a ten, fifteen-minute drive at most. We arrive at the party late. Me, Delvin and guy from Delvin's High School named Shooter. They had played football together and occasionally hustled together as well. The party itself is not talking about much, it's run of the mill. Not very crowded, not very exciting. As the night drags, we begin to see the signs that the party is about to come to an end. Delvin taps me.

"Let's go," He says, wearing his signature grin. The three of us leave, and we rush out to the vehicle in a bit of a tizzy. That's when

I realize that Delvin is rushing off to Phase 2. We jumped into the car, Delvin behind the wheel, Shooter in the back and me in the passenger seat.

This hotel differed from the Stadium Inn. As opposed to sitting at the end of a huge parking lot, the venue sat right on a rather busy three-lane street with a major freeway exit/on-ramp to the west of it, and a failed business sector and dwindling residential area far to the east of it. It was more motel than a hotel, as most of the rooms opened up directly to the warm summer air, as opposed to enclosed hallways. The layout was not ideal for stunt driving, swerving or yanking it, but we never really cared for the ideal.

The Blue Chew shot out of the parking spot and into the street in front of the hotel. Two years had passed since the epic and surreal night outside Stadium Inn and in that time our antics had not died now in the least. If anything, they had become more perfectly honed, all in pursuit of another Oochie Wally night, which to that point, had yet to be found.

There were no Nas songs playing this go around. Delvin zoomed down the street passing the hotel as the first group of teens begin to trickle out of the emptying venue. We pulled into a nearby gas station, turned around and sped back up the street passing the hotel again, this time braking hard and swerving in a bid to purchase attention with reckless car tricks that we had become so used to pulling off.

"Delvin drive like he damn Dale Earnhardt," Shooter said from the backseat.

"Mannnn, who you telling?" I clicked my tongue as I responded, agreeing with Shooter's sentiment. I sat leaned back low in the passenger seat, trying my best to pretend that the speeding, stopping and swerving were not disturbing or disconcerting to me in the slightest. I wasn't wearing a seat belt, as back then, we never wore seat belts.

"We gotta make one more pass through ya'll, just to stunt on'em one last time." Delvin could sense that Shooter and I were over phase two of this particular teen night and were ready to move on, "one more pass through" was his idea of a compromise. Neither me nor Shooter protested. He took the car out of sight of the hotel made a U-turn and started down the street again.

By this time the venue had completely emptied out. Everyone from inside the party was outside, and the traffic had begun to thicken with the regular civilian traffic of the area, as well as other departing partygoers, some as flashy and as reckless as us. We picked up speed, Delvin shook the wheel, and the car swayed and rocked from side to side. We screeched into the thick of the traffic, right in front of the hotel, this brought the eyes of everyone who had yet to reach their car on to us now, we could not disappoint. Delvin swerved out of the lane we were in, saw an opening, zipped between two vehicles, picked up speed, and swerved back into the previous lane. By the time I realized it wasn't as much space as we thought, Delvin was already mashing down the brake. Again, as it had so many times before, the car's tires screamed and screeched as they tried desperately to stop the vehicle from rolling forward.

The car in front of us wasn't moving, we were trying to stop, trying to brake, but there wasn't enough space and there wasn't enough time. The hood of the Blue Chew dipped down as the front wheels locked up and the brake pads clenched down hard onto the rotors. The car jerked, attempting to will itself to stop, our sudden change in speed lifted me from my seat, instinctively I braced one hand on the dashboard, assuring myself we would stop just in the nick of time as we always did, and my youthful strength would hold me steady until it happened. It did not. Sliding and slowing but still moving to fast, we slammed into the back of the car in front of us. The car stopped, but I kept going and for a brief moment I was airborne all over again, the same way that I had been when Delvin and I dived into that puddle years earlier, only this time there was no water to slide through, with a resounding "thwop" my forehead slammed against the windshield of Sweet's car. The impact created a large crack in the glass that spiderwebbed out in every direction and almost as quickly as I flew forward, I was slammed back down into my seat as if I were being slammed back down into reality. We sat for a moment in complete silence, stunned. Delvin looked at me, looked at the crack in the windshield, and then looked at my forehead. We both turned to look at the car in front of us that we had just rear-ended, and then thought in unison yet without words. "How in the fuck are we going to explain this?"

"Go Kinfolk Go Kinfolk!" Shooter yelled from the back seat, breaking both Delvin and me from our confused stupor. On-command, Delvin threw the car in reverse dislodging our front end from their rear end. Then he slammed the car back into drive, cut the wheel to the right and hit the gas so hard that the car screeched and screamed just as loud as it had before the crash. We shot off like a bullet out of the barrel of a gun.

The driver of the car that we hit was opening his door and getting out of his vehicle. I assume to survey the damage and exchange insurance information. Fuck that. Before he realized what was going on, we were halfway to the freeway. As we zoomed by, I saw him mouth the words "What the fu-?" and then hop back into his car in an attempt to come after us. It was no use, Delvin hit the interstate and vanished into a blur of headlights before he could fully regroup. He followed us onto the freeway, but we lost him within a mile and a half. A part of me breathed a sigh of relief that we had ran into a young guy who still had the wherewithal and sensibility to hop back in his car and try and chase us down. I'd hated the idea that we had rear-ended some little old lady and then smashed off leaving her with a crashed car and whiplash. I was a hoodlum, yes, but I liked to think I was at least a hoodlum with a heart of gold.

"Slowdown Delvin, you lost him. You gon get into another wreck trying to get away," Shooter called out again from the back seat, apparently, the only one of us completely comfortable and level headed in high-speed car chases.

"I'm just making sure," Delvin eeked out a nervous laugh, I could tell he was a little shaken up. He looked over at me, "You straight Nate?"

"Yeah I'm good," I respond, a little shaken up myself.

"I thought you cracked your damn skull open on that windshield man, you ain't even got a scratch. Hard-headed ass." He let out a real laugh this time. I laughed too. What else was there to do.

There is a phrase we use in my community that goes "got it out the mud," it means you built something from nothing in the most difficult way possible. When you put "we" in front of that phrase, it means "we" built something from nothing in the most difficult way possible, it means when no one else believed, we believed, and we held fast to those beliefs and together we trudged and crawled through dirt and grime to reach a shared goal or level of achievement. Yeah, me and Delvin, we got it out the mud.

Always wear your seatbelt, never let teenagers drive.

<u>Hey Love,</u>

I met my wife in a library, introduced to her by an English Teacher. That's oddly poetic to me, for a wannabe writer to meet the love of his life in such a way.

If the me of today were to hop into a time machine and go back and visit the 16-year-old me of yesterday, and as myself, I told myself, "Today we will meet that woman, that you will marry." I probably would not have believed me. That is, right up until I stepped into that library and heard her laugh, at that moment I would have believed everything I had taken the time to tell myself. There would not have been a single doubt.

In truth, it begins with the English Teacher. I was in high school, in my eleventh-grade year, when we got a new English teacher, Mrs. Poore. Throughout my high school career, I was a bit of a bastard. I was a "C" student who fell into the classic category of, "If only he would just properly apply himself, he could be a 'B,' or maybe even an 'A' student." But to apply oneself was a bore, to crack jokes and make the entire class, or at least a respectable section, burst out into spontaneous laughter, felt like a much more rewarding use of my time. That in addition to the fact that I played football, ran track and ran with a street crowd, my ideal self-image didn't really leave much room for "applying oneself." I imagine I was a bit more arrogant than the average student. I had a decently natural intelligence that allowed me to get by with only the minimal amount of effort, and that's just what I did and planned to continue to do right up until graduation. I was quite literally, to cool for school.

Needless to say, when the school year started Mrs. Poore, and I had quite the adversarial relationship. I was being kicked out of class daily, for making jokes and other random outbursts. But over time she warmed up to me and soon became my favorite teacher and in some ways like a second mother.

In the spring of my junior year, my new favorite teacher decided to take on a number of tasks that she felt were necessary for the betterment of my overall well-being. The first of which, was that I join the Forensics team and the second was that I find a girlfriend, someone that would provide a counterbalance to my wild and outrageous ways and encourage me to grow and mature. She decided that she would be the official matchmaker.

For Mrs. Poore, Forensics was an easy sell, it was an afterschool activity that was a combination of debate club and competitive drama, and for most, it would have been a reputation killer, but I had it in my head that I was beyond reproach and that there was little to nothing that could hurt my reputation. It's not that I was necessarily popular, just arrogant, oh so arrogant.

The matchmaking, on the other hand, was a different story. Mrs. Poore would list off respectable female students that I would then proceed to shoot down left and right for no reason other than she suggested them. And then one day we were headed to a meeting for the forensics team, I had been dodging the meetings up until that point, but Mrs. Poore had finally cornered me and forced me to keep my word about joining the team. I reluctantly followed her to the library, kicking myself for making the commitment in the first place.

"I'm going to have to introduce you to Marsha, I would say you two would make a good match, but you may be too silly for her. She is very mature for her age, and you are not."

I shrugged off this comment. "Works for me." I thought to myself, happy to have the understanding that everyone's expectations had been properly set. "I am both immature and childish and will, therefore, be doing the minimal amount of work and putting forth the most minimal amount of effort."

We entered the library which was for the most part empty, as it was after school hours and the only students that remained in the building would have been the basketball team, and none of them were in the library. Mrs. Poore and I made our way across the room to a table in the corner, sitting there waiting for us to arrive, was a girl. Dark brown skin, long hair and round full lips that pulled back into a bright and honest smile as we approached. She looked up at us with these ancient Nubian eyes. Immediately I knew that I had seen her around school before, but we had never really spoken to one another. We had kind of been in two different worlds, and there had never been a need to. She was all Advanced Placement and Honors Classes, Marching Band, and Girl's Track. I was barely a "C" student in gen pop, all football and rap notebooks. I was one of the guys that never took anything seriously; a resident class clown. Mrs. Poore was right, we might have made a good match, but we were too different, we must have passed each other in the halls a hundred times over the past two and a half years, and neither of us gave the other a second look.

I sat down, grinning happily to know that if I was going to be stuck on the forensics team at least, it was with someone pretty to look at. Though the chances of us getting along were low according to what Mrs. Poore had said about our maturity levels. While most of the kids in general population found me funny, or at least likable, the honors students, in particular, the girls, did not. Our teacher and Forensics coach made introductions and commented on how we would be working together on a scene from a very famous play. She made another jab at me, the specifics of what she said I can't remember, but it was probably something to try and make me feel embarrassed. I responded with a quick and witty retort, a random joke in reply to the teacher's teasing, I couldn't for the life of me tell you exactly what I said, but I know it must have been funny because Marsha burst out laughing. Genuine and joy-filled laughter as if she had been surprised not only by what I said but by how much she enjoyed it. Her laugh echoed through the small section of the library we were sitting in, and I smiled, and I stared at her and in that moment, in that singular defining moment, so much of my future had been solidified.

I'd like to think within that library, some time-traveling future version of myself was peeking out from around a bookshelf; observing that moment, hearing the joke and hearing her laugh. Then looking down to a crumpled picture of an empty landscape, the future me would see images of my teenage and young adult children appear in crisp and startling clarity as if they had been a part of the picture all along.

I am attempting to convey to you the gravity of this moment, but I know I cannot truly do it justice. The discovery of a dead body, the soul gratifying punch landed on the jaw of a bully, dodging gunfire, diving head first into a puddle of rainwater with your best friend. These are all moments in my life that have helped shape and define who and what I am. As this young brown girl's laughter echoed through the half-empty library of my high school, the clockwork gears of time and space paused for one elongated moment, freezing the universe in its place just long enough for it to be written in some unseen ledger by some unseen force, that I had just met the love of my life. A man's life is nothing, if not a series of moments; moments that begin and end in an instant, and other moments that echo into forever.

I shook myself out of my momentary daze, both taken aback and pleasantly surprised by her reaction to whatever it was that I had said. The meeting continued; lead by Mrs. Poore, with a few more jokes thrown in by me and a few more laughs thrown in by Marsha. A week or so passed and we begin to study and practice the scene that Mrs. Poore had in mind for us. It was a scene from the play "Fences" by August Wilson. We practiced and practiced for weeks, and after a time, we were set to have our first Forensic meet.

A forensic meet is very different from athletic competitions, it's inside the school for one, and there are no fans or supporters present, everything is done solely amongst the competitors and their judges. Marsha and I walked into a classroom full of students. They were fraternizing and talking to one another, being social. While me and Marsha strolled in with our noses in the air, speaking to or acknowledging no one. We were called up to perform our scene first. We went up to the front of the class and proceeded to completely and horrifyingly bomb. We stood in the front reciting our memorized line smiling at each other and holding back laughs the entire time. We barely made it through the scene. I can only imagine the awkwardness that we put the rest of the room through as we stood there making goo-goo eyes at one another the entire scene. The group that went second wiped the floor with us, it wasn't even close.

After that first meet, we vowed to do better, and while flipping through one of our school textbooks, I found a scene from the play "Barefoot in the Park" by Neil Simon. The characters reminded me of the sitcom "Mad About You" a show about a married couple that both Marsha and I watched and loved. We practiced the new scene on our own, determined to execute to perfection in our next Forensics Meet. We never had another Forensics Meet, but we continued to practice our "Mad About You" inspired scene until the end of our junior year.

The summer came, and without the excuse of school or forensics to put us together, Marsha and I were separated. That summer I was working in a sneaker store in Rivergate Mall. While I'm standing there counting down the hours until my shift was over, in walks my scene partner. She had come to the mall with her older brother.

"Hey," I said, as she moseyed up to me with a grin.

"Hey," she responded.

I stared at her for a moment simply smiling and not speaking then quickly broke the silence before it became too awkward.

"Are you ready for school to start back?" I asked.

"Yeah I am, are you going to do Forensics again this year."

"Yeah probably, " I said rubbing the back of my head, "Otherwise I'm sure Mrs. Poore won't leave me alone about it."

Her smile widened. "Well I need to get some new shoes for school, can you help me?" she asked.

We talked for another fifteen minutes, about plans for senior year and about sneakers in the store she liked and didn't like. She ended up choosing a pair of blue and silver Nike Air Max Specter, size seven and a half.

School started back in the fall, and the two of us began right where we had left off at the end of last year, and before long we were wrapped up in the throes of the Teenage Black Love Process. We began having long drawn out phone conversations that would last from late in the evening until the sun was breaking on the horizon the next day. More than once I fell asleep with the phone to my ear, reluctant and at times blatantly refusing to hang up, even though we knew we would see each other in school the next day. Yet and still, with all of those late-night phone calls, we were technically "just friends." Until a late night in November near the end of the first semester of our Senior year.

Marsha and I were on the phone as it drifted later and later into the evening. We used to play this game that we aptly named the Scenario Game, in which one of us would throw out some type of scenario, and we would then have a conversation as if the scenario was our reality. I can't recall what the particular scenario was on that night, but I do remember when it went off the rails.

The scenario game leads us to a point of disagreement and Marsha made her move.

"So, tell me how you really feel about me?"

"Excuse me," I said, almost choking on my own words.

"How do you really feel?" she repeated. Firm and without hesitation.

I cursed under my breath, the Scenario Game had been an emotional safety zone that allowed us to freely express feelings of affection and intimacy toward one another without the fear of rejection or embarrassment. Anything said within the realm of the game that one might take as too bold or too forward could easily be recanted or dismissed merely as playing a role within the confines of the game. Marsha had just ripped back the emotional insulation. I was an exposed nerve, raw and in the open.

"Seriously?" I responded.

"Seriously," she replied.

Saying the word "seriously" before or after a statement was our code for complete and total honesty. It means "What I have said is the absolute truth, no joke, no sarcasm, no exaggeration."

I cursed under my breath once again. I was in a desperate situation, I was about to share honest and vulnerable feelings with a girl that I had loved since I first heard her laugh, she could crush me with a single response.

In retrospect, my fears and apprehension were completely unfounded and made little to no sense. We were talking on the phone daily. Smiling at one another all day at school and I had even rearranged my senior year class schedule just to get closer to her. I changed one of my electives and forced the front office to move to me into Mrs. Poore's Drama Class, just so that Marsha and I could have a class together. Of which, up until it was finalized, and I was officially moved to the class, Marsha asked me about the status of daily. So, the chances of her rejecting my advances were little to none, but in my 17-year-old mind, the emotional risk that this moment posed was all too real.

"Well I know for me, I like you. Like, 'like you' like you."

"Oh, Well I 'like you' like you too."

"Really?" I said in feigned ignorance.

"Why haven't you said anything before now?" she asked not letting me off the hook.

"I don't know," remember I'm seventeen and dumb.

"Well, now what?"

"Well maybe now we should become a couple," I said.

"Seriously?"

"Seriously," I replied.

Nine years later, precisely to the date, I married the girl that I met in the library. Mainly because she laughed at my jokes.

PART II: THE FICTION

Justice

We stood in an extremely long line that now lay behind me
and seemed to trail off into forever. The line lead into a large
open room with high ceilings similar to a gymnasium, or perhaps
an airplane hangar, it is hard to say which. The air hung heavy
with the smell of heat and sweat, of rubber and metal.

The immense room was sectioned off into different areas;
separated only by a consensual social contract upheld by
everyone present. The line we were standing in ran along the east
wall, while in the center of the room there stood a fairly large
open space, and along the west wall sat raised, tiered rows of
metallic benches, patiently awaiting an audience to watch some,
as of yet, unforeseen event.

On the wall furthest from the entrance stood 8 to 10 metal
body cast dummies, shaped like the head and torso of a man.
The metal dummies gave off an intense heat, like opening an
oven at 400 degrees without first preparing yourself for the
sudden change in temperature. A rubber dummy lay outfitted on
top of the metal cast dummy. The rubber was thick, like the
rubber from a car tire, and seemed completely unaffected by the
heat coming from directly beneath it. The heat itself seemed only
present to stop onlookers from loitering. It forced one to do their
duty and move quickly away from the dummies where prolonged
exposure to the heat was unbearable. Not necessarily harmful you

see, only highly uncomfortable, which kept the endless line moving with relative speed, serving its purpose to perfection and turning out to be quite ingenious.

My position in line, however, had yet to get to the dummies. At my place in line, we were picking up knives. Long sharp knives with dark wooden handles. They reminded me of the cooking knives my mother use to have when I was a child. I took my knife in hand, testing the sharpness of the tip of its metal blade versus the end of my fleshy finger. The knife won, pricking my fingertip and drawing a tiny speck of blood.

Placing the blade of the knife under my arm, I put the wounded finger in my mouth and shuffled along maintaining my position in line. As we got closer to the back of the room, I could see those that were positioned in front of me stabbing the rubber dummies with the knives we had just received. There seemed to be no mandatory or predetermined number of times we were supposed to stab the dummies, but it looked as if everyone was taking 3 to 4 stabs each. "Enough to show you meant it." Seemed to be the unwritten rule. I followed suit.

The stabbing of the rubber man felt grotesque. The rubber body felt by no means human; however, the feelings it recreated were the same. The stabbings were violent, and the cuts left in the rubber were jagged and distorted. The rubber would grab hold to the metal blade upon each thrust, forcing a participant to use greater strength and effort to pull the blade out of the rubber body. As a result, the following thrust was always executed with exponentially more viciousness and ferocity, as if stabbing the dummy harder would make retrieving the blade a bit easier, so by the third and fourth stroke even the most reluctant participant was stabbing like a well-experienced psychopath. Myself included.

My knife slid past the rubber and scraped the metal cast that lay underneath, sending a horrifying chill down my spine. I was struck with the most unbearable feeling, like fingernails on a chalkboard every time the two metals touched. After making my stabs, I quickly moved along to the bleacher-like seating set up along the west wall. Many others had already taken their seats after their turn with the dummies, knives still in hand.

I spotted my cousin Darryl, who had apparently been in line ahead of me. He was moving toward a set of bleachers not far from the back of the gym. It was not the best angle to see then open floor area in the middle of the room, which now seemed to be the new focus of the event, but it was my cousin and a familiar face, so I followed suit. I greeted Darryl, who looked glad to see me as always, and then took my place in the stands. From my seat, I could see, waiting in line after just getting his knife, Lance, an old schoolyard friend of mine that I had always enjoyed talking to and joking with. We played football together in primary school. He was a good guy and had been a good friend who I had not seen in, and I can admit I was excited to catch up with him on the time that had passed. I decided to flag him down once he had gotten closer to our seats so that he and his brother James, who was standing near him in line, could join us. As well, I figured I would also watch him stab the dummies. My seat was perfect for watching him go through the same motions that I had, and in all honesty, Lance and I always enjoyed competing with one another when given the opportunity.

Lance was big, and while he was not taller than me, he was much better built. We had begun school together at roughly the same size, but his unbelievable work ethic and dedication to sport had made him almost twice my size by graduation.

That was some time ago; however, his size and stern demeanor still gave him a very intimidating look. Lance, though very lighthearted and friendly, wore a permanent scowl on his face, as if he was always on the brink of losing his patience. It was perfect for the aggressive contact sports we played in school, and the stern facial expression seemed to be hereditary as his brother had the exact same look even though he was much smaller.

I watched, expecting Lance to stab the dummies viciously, with so much force that perhaps he'd even shear through the metal itself, but he did not. He hovered by the rubber dummies, but he never thrust his knife toward them. Instead, after everyone else had done their stabbing, he moved toward the center of the gym, his brother along with him, as did a few other people. Knives still in hand.

Behind them, a gray curtain dropped hiding the metal and rubber dummies and further emphasizing the open area in the middle of the room.

Lance and the others stepped into a white lined box that had been taped off in the middle floor. The squared arena looked to be about 25 meters on each side, and Lance his brother James and some 20 other men stood in a line on the northeastern edge. A female voice spoke clearly over a P.A. System from speakers that I could not see. The voice was warm and sweet, like honey.

"These men have been accused of crimes against the State. Murder, theft and treason, all crimes punishable by death." The voice rung out like a bell, each word enunciated with precision. "However," she continued, "because the State is an entity that is both fair and just, each of the Charged will be given the opportunity to be absolved. If they can survive the Cutting Trial, they will earn the right to be then tried individually."

At this, a few people removed themselves from the stands and entered the white square arena with the intentions on stabbing my former classmate. Their faces wore smug smiles as if proud to be the ones dispensing this twisted sense of justice. A whistle blew from the unseen speaker, and they began. The men danced around each other swinging the knives wildly. The Charged Men seemed to have no real strategy, only to remain uncut for as long as they could, for the other men, the ones doing the chasing, it was just the opposite. Every time a man was finally cornered and stabbed, he screamed out loudly, and every time my heart broke. My mind went back to the rubber dummy that I had stabbed earlier, and my stomach turned.

The Chasers came in a variety sizes and ages, and although they had not really outnumbered the Charged at first, as each of the accused men was stabbed, he seemed to disappear from the fray, and by now the Chasers outnumbered the Charged 2 to 1. They were wrangling the accused into corners and then one of the more nimble Chasers would slip past the frantic and panicked swings of a Charged knife and wrestle him down to the ground. They started by simply poking the Charged in an exposed arm or leg, drawing blood and therefore sealing their fate. But as the match progressed the Chasers seemed to grow more vicious and more ruthless. They did not need to stab the accused men to death, no, only an open wound was necessary, bleeding men were carried away by larger, heavily armed guards, who I had somehow, failed to notice before. The bleeding Charged were carried off, perhaps to their own private executions, to be stabbed as many times as the rubber dummies had been stabbed, I suppose. Making us all murderers in a sense, or at least that was what the feeling of guilt that churned inside me said. I leaned over to my cousin who seemed to be watching with no particular interest and spoke words that I knew should not be said.
"This... this isn't right."

My cousin hushed me with a slightly raised hand, "This is how things are." he replied. I could see his eyes dart nervously over to one of the armed guards as if checking to see if my complaint was overheard. The guard's eyes met Darryl's who then quickly looked away, focusing his attention back to the knife-wielding men in the arena.

Another man had just been stabbed. A Chaser had him pinned to the ground with his legs wrapped around the criminal's waist

and holding his torso tightly from behind, so he had nowhere to
move to. A young man with a Mohawk, who looked to be around
the age of 18 or 19, stood over them. He stabbed the criminal in
the ribs, looking down upon him with a feeling of extreme
delight. His smugness irritated me to no end, his look of
satisfaction after claiming the life of another in the name of
justice made hate swell within me. He reminded me of the State
Men, the armed guards and enforcers of our "unnatural law" and
my disdain for him grew even more.

By now the only man left was Lance. The Chasers began to
surround him, moving in reluctantly, his intimidation had reached
even them. But in my heart, I knew it would only last for so long.
I quietly wished that he would at least slash open the throat of
the young man with the Mohawk before the Chasers could get to
him. I hoped for it desperately.

What happened next, I will not say. In truth it is irrelevant.
Lance's capture or escape, his death or release, none of it really
matters. The damage had been done when the first knife had
been thrust into the first dummy. When we allowed for the first
man to be carried away his fate hanging by only a thread while
cruel men anxiously twiddled sharpened knives between their
fingers. When we allowed for a system of revenge labeled justice
to be the law of our land, but what could be done, like everyone
else I sat by, said and did nothing. Perhaps it is as my cousin said,
"this is how things are" this is our system for justice.

Goblin'd

Part I

Chapter 1 - Bedtime

"Time for bed buddy boy."

"Daddy, no! I don't wanna go to bed!"

Edward smiled at his son, "I know you don't Bud, but you have to go to sleep now so we can get up tomorrow and start a new adventure."

"An adventure?!" The small boy's eyes lit up at the mention of the word.

"Yes sir!" responded his father.

"Let's go on an adventure right now!"

Edward laughed. "Alex, we can go on an adventure tomorrow. Right now, we need to go to sleep."

"Can I sleep with you and Mommy?"

"No buddy, you need to sleep in your own bed, like a big boy."

"But what if something gets me?"

Edward laughed again, "Nothing is going to get you bud. I promise. Now hop on up in the bed, I'll tuck you in."

Alex threw his arm around his father's neck.

"I love you, daddy."

"I love you to bud, now let's get you under these covers."

Edward stood up with his son in his arms and laid him on the bed; covering him with a blanket decorated generously in a random assortment of dinosaurs.

"Goodnight daddy."

"Good night bu-" Edward took a step away from the bed and immediately heard a loud crack. Looking down, he saw a plastic toy airplane crushed under the sole of his bare foot. "Alex, what did I tell you about leaving your toys on the floor?"

Edward looked around his son's room. It was littered with toys. Superheroes, race cars and shape changing robots lay scattered across the carpet. He gathered up the toys with relative speed and dropped them into a half-empty toy box in the corner. Edward noticed a small round handle protruding from the pile of plastic action figures. He reached down, grabbed the handle and pulled a large wooden baseball bat from the box.

"Al, what is my bat doing in your toy box?"

Alex peeked from underneath his blankets, keeping his nose and mouth covered, leaving only his eyes and forehead visible.

"Sorry, Daddy..."

"Alex this is my bat from college bud, you know it's off-limits."

"I know daddy, but I needed to borrow it so I could practice baseball."

"Practice baseball?"

"So I can be as good as you one day."

Edward stared at the bat for a moment, then looked up at his son with a smile that, unbeknownst to him, can only be smiled in those rare father-son moments, when a son says to a father the very type of thing his son had just said to him.

"I'll tell you what bud, tomorrow we'll get you a bat of your own to practice with, and we'll take this one here, and mount it up on your wall."

"You mean I can have it?"

Edward took another look at the wooden baseball bat. It was covered in some eighteen scribbled autographs each with a number beside it. He let his fingers slide over the message etched into the wood that read:

'To Edward Polanco, a true leader both on and off the field.'

"Yeah bud, it's all yours," Edward said leaning the bat against a bookshelf that sat right next to the bedroom door. He stepped over to his son's bed and placed a hand on the boy's head.

"Sleep tight okay buddy."

"Okay daddy, I love you."

"I love you too bud, see you in the morning."

"See you in the morning daddy."

Edward kissed his son on the forehead taking an extra moment to inhale deeply, taking in the smell of him. Then, rustling his hair as he stood, Edward quietly made his way out of the room, switching off the light as he left. The room darkened from within but was then softly re-lit by the silver streaks of moonlight that filtered in through the bedroom window.

Edward left his son's room, and started down an open hallway, flicking light switches from the 'on' to the 'off' position as he went. First the hall, then the laundry room, then the den and then the bath. He walked past a set of stairs, that lead down to the first floor of the house, and into his own bedroom where a slender brown-skinned woman with shoulder length hair pinned into a bun was sitting on the bed with a book in her hand. She didn't bother looking up as he entered the room.

"What are we gonna do with your son?" Edward asked with a sigh and a simple smile.

"The two of you are something else," she replied, still not looking up from her book.

"I found my bat in his room... again."

The woman finally looked up from her book revealing an alarmingly attractive face.

"Your U of M bat?"

"Yep," Edward flopped down onto the bed next to her.

"Aw babe, your teammates gave you that bat for your final season."

"Yeah, I know, but Alex said he needs it to practice with so, " Edward couldn't help but giggle to himself once again. "I'm just gonna let him have it."

"Practice!? He's only 5 years old, what is he practicing?"

Edward laughed out loud. "His words, not mine."

"That boy really idolizes his father. He wants to be just like you."

Edward's smile faded away and was slowly replaced by a grimace.

"Nah, I'd much rather he be better than me." Edward clenched his right knee, kneading and massaging it with both hands. His wife noticed his apparent discomfort.

"Are you okay babe? Is your knee bothering you?"

"No, it's just a little ache-y."

"Well the news did say it was supposed to be a big storm tonight, you know the rain always seems to set your knee off."

Edward sighed, "Ang, that's an old wives' tale, the weather doesn't have any eff- "

"Excuse me?" Edward's wife cut her eyes sharply at him from her side of the bed. Edward stopped in mid-speech.

"Oh, Did I say, 'old wives' tale'? I meant to say that's a 'young wives' tale.'"

"Uh huh," She went back to her book.

"I meant to say that's a 'pretty young wives' tale.'"

"Yea, nice try."

Edward leaned over and kissed his wife on the cheek.

"I'm just going to go to sleep now."

"You'd better."

Edward leaned back on to his pillow.

"I love you, babe."

"You'd better."

And with a smile, Edward fell into a gentle sleep.

Part II

Chapter 2 - Goblin'd

It was the crash of thunder that woke Edward. The trembling and shuddering of the house that not only forced his eyes open but also forced his consciousness out of the dream world and back into a cold dark reality. It took a moment for his mind to catch up. To distinguish what was real and what was not. He could hear the rain, see the flashes of lightning, feel the rumbles of thunder. But then there was something else. Rustling from within the house sounds that were not part of the storm.

Shuffling, movement, maybe Alex was awake and stirring, or maybe... there was a thump, like the sound of something heavy dropping to the floor. The sound set off an alarm in Edward's mind, and he was out of bed and halfway across the dark bedroom before he knew it. He tried switching on the light to help him get his bearings, but the switch was unresponsive. The storm must have knocked out the power.

"Damn," Edward thought. Alex was probably terrified. Undoubtedly woken by the storm and had most likely fallen in his room while fumbling around in the dark. That had to be it. "But why hadn't he cried out? Why hadn't Alex called out for his mother or me." Edward rushed around to his son's room. The entire time attempting to reassure himself that he was overreacting, his parental instincts in overdrive. He had been this way since Alex was born. Even when he was an infant, Edward would wake in the middle of the night and sneak up to Alex's crib just to check that he was still breathing properly. It was silly, he knew, but what could it hurt. Always better to be safe rather than sorry. Angela teased him for dodding in this way, but he didn't mind, he had been teased about a lot worse in his 32 years and being an overprotective father was a badge of honor in his book. Edward made his way through the house, pass the stairs, the bathroom, the den, the laundry room and then down the small stretch of dark hallway to Alex's room. The entire house was practically void of light, leaving Edward's memory of his upstairs layout and a free hand on the wall to serve him in place of his eyes.

Edward stepped across the threshold into his son's room half expecting Alex to still be in bed sleep, either that or he would be on the floor of his room quietly weeping after having fallen in the dark. What Edward found instead was something else altogether.

Like the rest of the house, Alex's room was still dark from the lack of power, however, unlike any of the other rooms in the house, Alex's bedroom window was wide open allowing rain and wind to sweep into the room uncontested. As well, unhindered moonlight poured in through the opening and made the room glow with a silver luster. It was then that Edward saw it.

For an instant, he thought he was looking at an old man standing on his son's bed, but the thing's pale green skin betrayed any indication that it might be human. It was like a man... but not fully. It was more of a gaggle of bones and sinew poorly wrapped in sickly green leather. It was only about four feet tall, with gangly and twisted limbs that seemed slightly too long for its shriveled and wrinkled body. It was wearing nothing but a tattered scrap of brown cloth around its waist, from the bottom of which, thin stringy legs protruded and ended with dirty and gnarled feet whose jagged thick toenails looked like they had been purposely sharpened into claws. It was a creature. A grotesque little monster the likes of which Edward had never seen before. Startled, he took a step back, but then saw something else... Edward saw what the thing was holding.

Alex's limp body lay cradled in the creature's arms. The boy stirred, but before he could fully open his eyes, the monster pushed its face towards Alex's and opened its mouth releasing what looked toxic green fumes directly into the boy's face. Edward could see the green mist curl and sway before being inhaled straight into his son's nose and mouth, who upon breathing the monster's exhalation immediately went back limp. Upon witnessing this, Edward's mind snapped from a frozen state of mortified horror to an unyielding rage, and almost without thinking he reached down and grabbed the wooden baseball bat that lay leaning against the bookshelf.

"PUT HIM DOWN!!" Edward lunged forward swinging the bat savagely at the thing's head. The creature looked up for the first time, apparently unaware that Edward had been standing in the doorway up until that moment and in an unexpected show of agility the monster leaped backward off the bed and landed firmly on the window sill, with Alex still in his arms, and his eyes, now, duly fixed on Edward.

The creature was ugly, which Edward had already suspected, but it wasn't until he looked directly into the face of the thing that he realized exactly how hideous the beast was. The old man motif persisted throughout the monster's appearance. It's skin, weathered and beaten hung loosely from its face and a tuft of gritty black hair sprouted from the top of its skull. It stared at Edward with bulbous, yet penetrating eyes that seemed to glow a nightmarish yellow. Long pointed ears jetted out of either side of its head, while a large over-sized nose, hooked, broken and crooked, sat overtop a pair of thin black lips that were currently curled back to reveal teeth, all jagged chipped and stained. Then... without warning, the thing spoke.

"FiNd tReASure." It said with a voice that sounded like a tin fork scraping against a dinner plate. It was both raspy and high-pitched, "ClAiM wHaT iS pReCioUs, tAkE bAcK tO cLaN. THaT iS GObLiN wAy." Its words were hard and forced as if it were painful to speak. Edward winced at the receipt of each word as if it were also painful to listen.

"Goblin?" Edward responded more to himself then to the thing. "Is that what you are? A goblin?"

"niL'boG clAiMs hU-mAn tReASure. mAn NoT HiDe, mAn NoT PROtect. niL'boG cLAiM!" The goblin, Edward surmised, seemed to be getting agitated, and a thick white foam began to accumulate in the space between its gums and lips, gathering in mass around its rotten teeth, spittle flying from the mouth as it spoke with more and more enthusiasm.

"So you're Nil'bog... the Goblin? You want treasure? I can get you treasure, just... just put my son down. Okay?" Edward tightened his grip on the bat. Alex was still laying in the Goblin's arms, apparently fast asleep. He was watching closely and could see his son's chest rise and fall of its own accord. Perhaps the goblin's breath acted as some type of makeshift anesthetic to keep Alex docile and under control. Regardless he had to get the creature to put Alex down, and if the thing could talk, perhaps it could be reasoned with.

"niL'boG clAiM gReAtEsT tReASue," the goblin spewed, while at the same time throwing Alex over his shoulder like a sack of potatoes. "tAkE bAcK tO cLaN, niL'boG pRoVE niL'boG brAvEst, niL'boG stRoNGest. niL'boG nAmEd ChiEf," The Goblin thumped his chest with the free hand that was not holding Alex tightly to his pale green body. "iS GObLiN wAy!" The last three words Nilbog hissed out, his bright yellow eyes narrowing into thin slits of spite and enmity. Then he turned and jumped out of Alex's dormer window onto the surrounding roof and out into the night and rain.

"NOOOO!" Edward screamed dashing over his son's bed and to the now empty window sill. The goblin was still on the roof, still watching Edward, still choking out horribly broken English, while slowly walking backward closer and closer to the roof's edge. "ANGELA!" Edward screamed for his wife who came running into the room almost immediately, the previous commotion having already sent her on her way.

"What's going on?" she screamed in a desperate and confused panic.

"Something... a monster -- a goblin grabbed Alex! I have to go after him, call the police!" Edward refused to take his eyes off of Alex and the creature, he didn't bother looking back at his wife.

"A what!?! What grabbed Alex? Where is he?"

"ANGELA CALL THE POLICE, SOMETHING HAS GRABBED OUR SON, AND I HAVE TO GO AFTER IT!" Edward broke his vow and looked away from his son and back at his wife, his face painted in the color of rage and fear, hers only in fear and confusion. He looked back out the window to see the Goblin jumping from the roof. It had been waiting for Edward to break his line of sight and took full advantage of the opportunity. It was attempting to run. Edward flung himself out the window and on to the roof without a second thought.

Bat in hand, barefoot and wearing nothing more than cotton pajama pants and a white V-neck t-shirt. He hit the roof with tears in his eyes as his mind tried to process what was happening in that exact moment. A goblin has crawled into his son's room and was now trying to carry him off into the dark for reasons beyond his understanding. All he knew was that he could not let them get away; otherwise, he'd never see his son again.

The night wind was cold and unforgiving as it swept in and battered itself against Edward's under-dressed body. Raindrops pelted down soaking through his shirt almost instantly. The rain had already done its duty to the exposed roof as well. When Edward's uncovered feet made contact with the rain-drenched shingles, they immediately abandoned any idea of grip or traction. Ed slipped; his feet went up, and his body went down, slamming onto the wet roof and sliding towards, and then over, the edge. He fell off the roof, and his body hit the soft wet grass below with a resounding thud, knocking the wind out of him in the process.

His back took the brunt of the damage. The fall was a little over ten feet, and aside from a bit of dizziness from the jolt, and a bit of huffing and puffing from the air being knocked out of his lungs, Edward was convinced he was fine. He shook off the haziness and stared intently around his own backyard for any sight of his son and his captor. Through the rain and mental fog, he spotted a small green body carrying a boy over its shoulder, running through the grass and mud like an ape would. Bounding forward on two legs while using its free arm to help propel him along. Nil'bog was attempting to carry Alex away as fast as his little goblin body would take him, and he was heading out of Edward's backyard and into a dense patch of forest that lay behind their home.

Chapter 3 - The Chase

Before Edward he'd even gotten well back onto his feet, Nil'bog had leaped onto the top of, and then over, the backyard fence with what seemed like little effort. Ed used the bat to stable himself as he scrambled up from the grass and to the base of the six-foot fence that the four-foot goblin had just treated more like a minor hurdle than a major obstacle. Edward tossed the bat over, then grabbed hold to the fence and pulled himself up onto the top in one adrenaline-filled motion. The fence was digging into his gut as half of his body leaned toward the dark forest, and the other half dangled over his backyard. With the fall from roof still clear and strong in Edward's mind, he flipped himself over the fence head first, turning a full 360 degrees in the air and this time landing flat on his stomach in a large puddle of mud that splashed in every direction as his body hammered itself into the ground. "If you can survive a fall from a roof, you can survive a fall from a fence." his mind screamed into his ears forcing him to jump up from the mud almost as quickly as he had landed in it.

He pushed himself up to his hands and knees. Looking around he quickly found the bat laying not too far from his own point of contact. He threw himself toward it, grabbing hold to the wooden handle. At the same time, he both heard and saw the rustle of a nearby bush planted right at the edge of the forest. He grabbed the bat in both hands.

"Come out!" he yelled into the darkness. The night did not respond, but as if to quiet itself for his benefit, the rain seemed to let up. "Nil'bog! I know you're there! COME OUT!" His body shook as he screamed. He stood hunched over. Barefoot in the rain and mud, his head and eyes darted in each direction, often times, one unable to keep up with the other. He had only been outside for a few minutes, but he already looked almost unrecognizable from the man who had just been in his son's room. " I SAID COME OUT!!!"

From the suspiciously rustling bush shot out a maw of open teeth and mud-stained goblin claws. Nil'bog the Goblin thief was flying at Edward in fury of bites and slashes with the apparent intention of either biting into his face or clawing out his eyes. Though Edward had requested it, he was still surprised by the creature's attack, and the force of the barrage put him on his back. Placing the bat between them, and using the momentum of his fall, Edward was able to fling the flying goblin over his head and into fence they had both come over. It was quick thinking on Edward's part, and in an effort to maintain that pace, Ed flipped over onto his stomach and looked to the bush from which the Goblin had come. Laying there, as he had hoped, was a small boy, Alex was right there in the bush, left behind by his captor if only for a moment as it attempted to either scare off or cripple their pursuer. But the monster's plan had not worked, and Edward's son was in sight.

The father scrambled forward still on his hands and knees attempting to get to his son. He was almost within arm's reach of the boy's ankle when he felt a sharp, and forceful push into his back that sent him once again face down into the mud. As he looked up, he could see the goblin jumping from off his back and into the bush that held his son, and almost as quickly as he had appeared. Nil'bog had scooped Alex up once again and took off into the dark woods. Edward cursed the goblin under his breath, stood up and begin to give chase.

The rain, which had been a curse to Edward's efforts when he was slipping and falling off of his roof, had become somewhat of blessing now that he was running barefoot through mud and wet grass of the forest floor.

The rain had slowed to nothing more than a light drizzle, but the previous downpour had already soaked into the earth making the ground soft and pliable. The thick mud was caked at the bottom of Edward's feet offering him just enough protection to sprint through the undergrowth as if he was wearing running shoes. He would step on the occasional rock or pebble or even the randomly placed sharp twig, but whatever pain the layers of mud did not dull, the massive amounts of adrenaline being dumped into his bloodstream eradicated. The woods, he knew, would go on for another three to four miles before they would hit another shore of civilized society. He was wading deeper and deeper into a sea of undeveloped land. He had imagined that this makeshift wilderness would serve to aid his son's childhood, a place to explore and discover, hunt frogs and chase squirrels, build tree forts and secret clubhouses. All the things he wished he had the space to do as a kid, somehow, that had all gone horribly and terribly wrong. Now all of the chasing and hunting was being done by him, and sadly not for the betterment of his son, but instead, for the sake of him.

Nil'bog was a lot faster than he was, but it appeared that even goblins had limits and carrying around a small boy who weighed roughly forty-five pounds when the creature itself couldn't have weighed more than sixty, kept the goblin down to a pace that Edward could at least keep up with. Nil'bog tried his best to pull away. The monster bounded through the forest with aggressive and intimidating agility. It darted over and under bushes and fallen log with relative ease. It would dash between and around trees, turning and twisting in ways Edward did not think was possible. The goblin ran with its whole body, still using its free hand as a third leg, it pattered through the mud unimpeded by the things like ground suction or slipperiness. It would jump and swing from low hanging branches, reach out and grab tree trunks to offer itself assistance in making those unsavory turns, and then to add insult to injury, it would randomly sling mud and stones over its shoulder in an attempt to blind or impair Edward whenever the opportunity presented itself. It ran as if it were used to being chased. Regardless Edward was undeterred.

He hounded the goblin's heels with an ungodly determination. He pounded and splashed his way through the forest floor, intermittently releasing guttural screams and yells as he forced his body forward through the cold, wet wind. His arms, legs, and chest all burned as if his blood had been replaced with hellfire. He could hear and feel his heart beating in his ears. His breath ragged and mean in between his feral and primitive grunts. He gripped the barrel of the wooden bat tightly in his right hand while his left waded out in front of him constantly clawing at the goblin just out of his reach, and also knocking away flying debris and the random assortment of small branches that seemed to appear out of nowhere. The forest was dark, and navigation by sight was nearly impossible; however, there seemed to be just enough moonlight shining on the goblin's small frame to keep it in Edward's vision, and that was all he needed. As long as he stayed close to the Nilbog he could take the same path that he took, Edward may not have been able to see in the dark light of the moon, but the goblin had seemed to be doing just fine.

Part III

Chapter 4 - Confrontation

The trio twisted and turned deeper and deeper into the forest until suddenly, without warning, the trees stopped, and Edward found himself chasing the goblin through a wide open field. They were in a clearing, and now with no trees to dash between or around, Edward finally had the upper hand on the goblin. Its stride had weakened, and it was no longer moving nearly as fast as it was before. Carrying all of that extra weight had caught up to it and now it would either have to drop the boy to avoid being caught or simply stop altogether. Edward saw his chance. He reached down into an unknown part of himself and mustered up the energy to close the distance between him and the monster. His legs pumped as hard as they ever had as he bounded through the grass. He reached out his hand, once again his son so close he could almost touch him, and then it appeared at the edge of his vision, and for the first time since he began the chase, Edward purposefully slowed down, and then stopped.

Across the clearing, at the edge of where the forest began again. Ahead of Edward, ahead of Alex, and ahead of the goblin Nil'bog, flames flickered. Not wild, unchecked flames. No, that would have at least partially made sense to Edward. These were small controlled flames, flames from a campfire, no more like a bonfire. Beyond the flames, reaching up to the night sky like a bony hand bursting forth from the earth and attempting to strangle the moon itself, was a tree. A gnarled and twisted tree that stretched and curled upward like the smoke that floated up the base of it. The tree, massive and grotesque, looked almost more like it was actually two trees that had twisted themselves together over the many years that they had grown there. It's black limbs splayed out into every direction, and its branches were covered in broad dark leaves that rattled like dead men's bones every time the wind blew. While the other trees swayed in the breeze brought on by the receding storm, the twisted twin trees seemed to go into violent convulsions that reminded Edward of the hunched over fits of coughing and hacking one would expect of someone on their death bed. Behind the bonfire, Edward could see twisted roots of the tree which plunged into both earth and stone like skeletal fingers in graveyard dirt. The tree grew on a mound, or a hill of some sort and upon the side of which, between its gnarled and twisted roots, there was a gaping hole, forming a cave entrance that looked more like the giant open mouth of a monster than a naturally occurring land formation.

Edward stood there, staring up at it, a monstrous tree whose disfigured roots had literally ripped a hole into the earth, forming a cave, that for all Edward knew, was a portal to an entirely different world. The flames from the bonfire flickered and rolled, randomly casting its light into different directions, cracking and popping in the dead silence of the night. Everything was still; even Nil'bog had stopped running, and it was then that Edward saw them. Thirty... no, forty glowing yellow eyes materialized in the darkness. And then the wind began to whisper, sputtering out words in much the same forced way that the goblin did when Edward first heard it speak.

"niL'boG hAs rEtURneD."

"hE hAs REturNeD?"

"niL'boG."

" hAs rEtUrNED...."

The wind whispered in a medley of different voices that seemed to surround Edward from every direction.

"niL'boG hAs bRoUGht trEaSuRe"

"TrEaSuRe!"

"SOmEthInG pReCioUs?"

The voices ricocheted off one another and cut through the air like bullets in a firefight, it was impossible to tell where they were coming from, or in which direction they were going. Nil'bog laid the still unconscious Alex at the base of the fire. Edward was now close enough to see that a number of other things lay around the fire as well. Trinkets, jewelry, rings, and watches, but then there were also scraps of clothing, half-eaten pieces of food, a number of indiscernible broken things and even a few dead animals. It was like someone had rustled through a hundred garbage cans and dropped what they had found here.

Nilbog stood over Alex hunched and wheezing still exhausted from his run. "niL'boG hAs bRouGHt gReAtESt trEAsUre. niL'boG hAs pRoVEn, niL'boG sHaLL bE nAmEd-"

"NO!" A thicker even raspier voice cut in, silencing Nil'bog's speech. Edward instinctively tightened his grip on the wooden bat. From behind the flames and out of the mouth of the cave another creature slowly stepped forward. It looked similar to Nil'bog; however, this creature was markedly older and considerably more decrepit. It wore a shroud over half of its body as opposed to just a simple Lyon cloth and it was also adorned with an assortment of necklaces made from beads, shells and other odd baubles. It leaned feverishly on a crooked stick that was as long as its body, and its nose and ears drooped, apparently weathered down by the passage of time. It looked like a fiendish Dalai Lama, and its sudden appearance made Edward scowl.

"niL'boG tHe NameLess ONe, yOu hAve brOUght dishOnOr to our clAn. niL'boG the NameLess hAs brOught MAN!" the old goblin spoke English much better then either Nil'bog of the disembodied voices that whispered into the wind, but this offered little comfort to Edward as the old Goblin's eyes looked down on him with a disdain that Edward had grown all too familiar with.

"niL'boG hAs bRoUgHT mAn!"

"mAn?!"

"niL'boG!" the voices whispered.

Edward stepped forward, he held the bat in one hand and with the other he motioned toward his son. "I've only come for the boy, let me take him and we'll go, we'll leave."

The old goblin seemed to ignore Edward altogether.

"niL'boG hAs brOugHt shAme to clAn, niL'boG hAs brOUght mAn to sAcrEd trEE. niL'boG hAs brOught dAnger to aLL GOblins."

"I'm no danger to you, I only came for my son!" Edward said, trying foolishly to interject reason into a situation he himself could make no logical sense of.

"niL'boG hAs brOught shAme to scAred trEE, GOblins mUst appEAse grEat trEE, grEat trEE mUst hAve blOOd."

"What?" said Edward.

The old goblin placed its withered hand on the root of the tree that protruded near the cave entrance. "GOblins kIll mAn, kIll bOy, trEE appEased... It iS GOblin wAy."

"What!"

"kiLL mAn," said the wind.

"kiLL bOy," the wind replied.

"FOr sACrEd trEE," the wind added.

"iT iS gObLiN wAy," as the wind spoke the whispers slowly started to take shape. The glowing yellow eyes begin to move in closer crawling out of the dark corners of the field revealing themselves to be monsters of the same build as Nil'bog. Goblins, dozens of them began to pour out of every available shadow.

"kiLL mAn."

"kiLL bOy."

"FOr sACrEd trEE."

"iT iS gObLiN wAy."

The goblins begin to slink toward Edward, crawling like slow-moving lizards across the ground, their voices still slithering through the wind like snakes without bodies. He took a step backward, setting his feet. He dug the ball of his right foot into the moist grass, bent his knees. He let the bat swing freely toward the ground then lifted it up to his ears gripping it with both hands, tightly, but not too tight. He held his right elbow high, strong, his biceps flexed. The goblins scurried closer, they were moving faster now, frantic and excited, thirsty for blood. Edward took a deep breath. The nearest goblin lunged at him, and like a programmed machine his body reacted. His left shoulder dropped, his left foot rose slightly off the ground, his hip torqued, he stepped out to the lunging goblin ripping the bat around him so fast that the solid wood turned into a wispy blur, right up until it connected with the head of the over-anxious fiend. Meeting the monster's skull with a loud "Thwack!" The goblin went somersaulting backward, flying through the air and flipping two or three times before landing on the ground motionless.

For a brief moment the goblins froze, they looked back at their motionless brethren that now lay on the ground just a few feet from the bonfire and the mouth of the cave. Its head split open and leaking dark green fluid. Then they looked back at

Edward, then back at their friend, and for a moment even the elder goblin looked stunned. But not Edward, he was done being stunned, or shocked, or surprised or confused. Now he was just angry.

"I'VE COME FOR MY SON, AND NONE OF YOU ARE GONNA STAND IN MY WAY!!!" Edward screamed at the top of his lungs, his every muscle flexed and then bulged as his body once again dumped even more adrenaline into his bloodstream.

The goblins seemed jolted back into action by Edward's war cry, and they once again begin to dash towards him even more fervently than before. The goblins lashed out with their clawed hands while bearing sharp crooked teeth. Edward swung the bat like a club swatting away goblin after goblin as the lunged at him. A downward slash caught one in the back of the head, nailing its face into the dirt. An upward swing caught another goblin under the chin, audibly shattering the bones in its jaw before sending him heels over head into the dirt. One goblin managed to land itself on to Edwards back, digging its claws into his torso and gleefully sinking its teeth into this right shoulder. Edward screamed out in pain, banged the bat against the goblins unprotected head, then reached back and yanked the creature over his shoulder onto the ground and brought the bat down onto the goblin's head two more times for good measure. There was a loud and audible splat as dark green goo flew out in every direction. Another goblin grabbed Edward's leg and took a bite, he growled and hit the thing with the butt of the bat handle, a random claw swiped him across the cheek, blood trickled down the side of Ed's face but did little else to slow his movement. The goblins had numbers, but their bodies seemed weak and frail under the weight of Edward's rage.

Though regardless of how many he struck down, the monsters kept coming. At one point between the vicious swings of the bat and the occasional goblin bite, Edwards looked up to see three goblins moving in on Alex, who still lay passed out by the bonfire. With a primal roar, Edward shook off at least two of the goblins that had latched on to him and begin to barrel toward his sleeping son.

"DON'T YOU TOUCH HIM!" Edward screamed, and at the same time the bat came down like a guillotine, crushing the neck of one of the goblins standing over Alex. The other two jumped out of range of the bat, redirected their efforts, and jumped on to Edward instead, joining the other odd number of goblins that he had not already managed to shake off. The only goblin who was not actively trying to kill either Edward or Alex was Nil'bog, who was still sitting in the same position that he was in when he was being scolded by his elder. He looked like a heart-broken child, sitting on his knees and staring blankly down at the dirt, seemingly completely oblivious to the chaos going on around him.

The goblins had thoroughly latched on to Edward now, there was scarcely a part of him that was not in some way covered by a pale green goblin body. As quickly as he could throw one off of himself, another would jump up to take his place. That's when the ones close to his head had begun to do something peculiar. They started retching and hacking. Their little green heads would bob, and a couple of seconds later they would burp, or at least it seemed like a burp. The goblins would open their mouths and exhale a misty green gas from the back of their throats, spewing it into Edward's face. Ed breathed in the green mist with little regard at first. His focus had been more concentrated on ripping the biting and clawing little monsters from his back and legs, but after a while, he felt his body becoming heavier and more sluggish and then he thought about what Nil'bog had done to Alex in his bedroom and realized the goblins were trying to knock him out. Since they could not overpower him, they were apparently planning to use their goblin's breath to do to him what Nil'bog had done to Alex. He could feel his head start to spin.

Even the biting and scratching felt less and less painful as goblin after goblin released green mist into his face. He looked down at his son, still sleeping serenely by the fire, still untouched, still protected. Edward lurched forward, his eyes now focused on the flames that burned before him, the only thing between him and them was the solemn and silent Nil'bog.

"Nil'bog," Edward thought, the cause of it all. He couldn't imagine that he could last too much longer with the goblin's constantly breathing in his face and the only thought that he could hold steady in his mind was that if he were to go down, he would take with him, as many of these little bastards as possible. And Nil'bog would be one of them. He took another step forward. Closer to the fire, closer to Nil'bog. The goblins held on tightly; they pushed and pulled trying everything they could to stop his movement. He advanced one more step, Nil'bog was in reach, he stuck his arm out. If he could grab him, he could simply fall forward into the flames, crush Nil'bog in the process and let the fire burn the goblins that were holding on too tightly. If he was lucky maybe he'd only suffer minor burns and if he could hop up fast enough, maybe he could grab Alex and run. If he were not lucky, well, at least they would all burn together. Edward reached out further, his vision darkened, his arms grew heavy, his knees buckled. The weariness was beginning to catch up with him, he was tired, and he was hurt. He dropped the bat which landed with a thud at his feet. He fell down to one knee, and the goblins piled on top of him. He tried to stand back up. But the monsters were too heavy, he dropped down on to all fours, his hands now in the mud, struggling to hold him up. His knee started to throb with pain, but not the pain of goblin bites and scratches, not the pain of running or exhaustion, but old pain, pain from an injury long ago, a pain of things lost in past lives, a pain of "could have been," and "what would not be," and in that pain he began to think. For some reason, he thought about that stupid bat, his bat... no. Not his bat, not anymore. Alex's bat. His son's bat, a bat that had been given to him as a reminder of the past, that he had given to his son as a reminder of the future. A reminder of hope and new dreams. A reminder of a father's promise to a son. A promise to teach and to protect and to guide.

Edward felt one more burst of strength, not of adrenaline, not even of rage but simply a strength of necessity, because a father must do what is necessary. Like a bomb, Edward burst forth sending little green goblins flying in every direction. He grabbed hold to the bat once again, his eyes finding Nil'bog still sitting in the same position as he rose his weapon. He squeezed every muscle in his upper body and then...

"sToP!" The elder goblin called out in his crooked and twisted voice. He banged his stick into the dirt and a wave of muffled green light irradiated from the ground beneath his feet, washing over everything in the clearing. Edward froze, bat still raised in the air, his body paralyzed, completely unable to move. The goblins around him froze. All movement had stopped in that instant.

"mUch GOblin blOOd hAs bEEn sPiLLed tHis nAme dAy." The old goblin looked up at the twisted branches of their tree. Then looked down at Edward, still frozen in place, covered now in mud and blood, his clothes ripped and torn and his eyes, full of rage and desperation. Broken goblin bodies lay all around him, splats of their sickly green blood seeped into the soil, mixing with water from the fresh rain.

"tHe sAcrEd trEE hAs bEEn aPPeaSed. mAn mAy tAke bOy, tHey mAy gO." And without another word, he grabbed his stick and crept back into the mouth of the cave among the roots of the goblin tree.

The other goblins followed suit dashing back to the base of the tree, lifting and dragging the others that could not move on their own. Within moments the goblins had gone, and only Edward, Alex and Nil'bog remained.

The lone goblin looked up for the first time since the fighting had started, his yellows eyes staring into Edward's. "niL'boG fAiLed, niL'boG unworthy..."

Whatever force that was holding Edward released him and he found himself able to move once again. He looked down at the goblin, and in one fluid motion slammed the butt of the baseball bat's handle into the goblin's forehead. The goblin collapsed to the ground with a thud, unconscious but still breathing. Edward picked up his son and began walking away from the tree back toward the forest. Over the crest of trees, he could see the sun starting to rise as the sky slowly began to lighten from a deep dark blue to a lighter morning shade of cobalt. Alex stirred in his arms. Waking for the first time, completely unaware of everything that had taken place.

"Daddy," the boy yawned "Where are we going?"

"Hey buddy, we're going home."

Alex didn't bother opening his eyes but instead snuggled up to his father's muddy chest.

"Daddy?"

"Yeah, bud?"

"Are we still going to go on an adventure?"

Edward smirked.

"Yeah bud, you and me, we're gonna go on plenty of adventures."

The End.

In Sheep's Clothing

Part I

Damien Sills Jr. sat alone in the driver seat of his black four-door sedan. A raspy voice whispered to him the lyrics of a song that he had heard at least a hundred times before. The music rolled and curled through the interior of the vehicle like smoke from a cigar or cigarette. The volume was low, yet and still, the vibration from the bassline could still be felt in the body of any pedestrian that may happen to wander to close to the dark car. For Damien, this was not a concern. There would be no pedestrians in this part of town, not at this hour.

Damien's car sat parked in an alleyway between, St. Andrew's Cathedral, an old and abandoned church, and the Belter Plant, a dilapidated and unused warehouse that used to be a sewing machine factory. Both buildings lay on the edge of New Hampton's Industrial district. Incidentally the industrial era of New Hampton had long passed, and as a result, an entire portion of the city lay desolate and decaying. No pedestrians ever wandered here, there was no reason too; this party of the city had become useless to most of New Hampton's residents, all except a few. Damien reached forward and cut the radio off altogether. The music, though already low, was beginning to become a distraction.

Damien was waiting for something, and there were few things he hated more than waiting. He checked his phone. No calls. No text. The time read 1:00 AM. He craned his neck to look through the windshield and up at the night sky to see a full moon that seemed to be sending the beams of its solar reflected light directly down onto him.

"Looks like God got you under the spotlight." He mumbled to himself, and for a moment he thought about moving his car. He dismissed the thought. No, he was where he should be. There was no need to move.

He heard a howl. Distant but strong, full like the moon itself, primal like a howl should be. Probably an old dog. He looked back out at the moon and thought how he had never actually seen a dog howl at the moon. He had seen plenty of dogs, seen plenty of moons and heard plenty of howls, but never had all three events occurred simultaneously before him. He wondered if it were true. About dogs howling at the moon, maybe dogs just howled because they were dogs. Who is to say they needed the moon? Damien rechecked his phone. No calls. No text. 1:02 AM. God he hated waiting. Damien slid his finger across the face of his phone, tapped in a four-digit code and pressed the first name listed on the speed dial. The phone rang... and rang. Damien took a deep breath, both inhaling and exhaling his frustration. Someone picked up.

"What up doe?" said a voice on the other end of the line.

Where ya at?" Asked Damien impatiently.

"Where you at?"

"I'm at the spot fool! Behind the church."

"Aight we down the street."

"Aight."

"Aight."

The phone conversation ended with a beep.

"Bruh ain't never on time," Damien mumbled to himself. He found that he mumbled to himself a lot when waiting for someone or something, hence his hate for the action, or more appropriately, the inaction of waiting. He took the time to scroll through the other features on his phone. Social network accounts, email messages, voicemails. Nothing new. He looked over to the passenger seat. There was a backpack, his. He grabbed the bag and placed it into his lap, unzipped it and reached inside. Damien pulled from the pack a wad of twenty-dollar bills, rolled tightly into a small knot and secured with a rubber band that appeared to have been doubled over numerous times to keep itself and the bills neatly in place. There were 50 bills within the roll, one thousand dollars in all, and within the bag, there were forty-nine others exactly like it. Damien dropped the money roll back into the bag and reached inside once again. His hand pushed passed the bundles of cash and hit something else within the backpack. Something cold and metal. Damien pulled a .45 semi-automatic pistol from his bag. He cocked the gun revealing a bullet waiting silently in the exposed chamber. The brass shell casing shimmered in the moonlight. Damien released the slide, and the gun's barrel chamber slammed shut with the defining clicks and clinks of the firearms mechanical pieces abruptly moving back into their rightful places. He zipped the backpack closed and placed it back into the passenger seat while putting the handgun into his lap. He closed his eyes and let his head fall back on to the seat's headrest and took another deep breath.

Damien felt a wave of light wash over him accompanied by the sound of gravel crunching under tires. He didn't bother to open his eyes. The car pulled in next to him, he heard doors open, low mumblings, indistinguishable words and then doors closing. Immediately his own passenger door flung open.

"Wake up fool!"

Damien opened only his right eye and peered over to see a smiling face remove the backpack from the passenger seat and replace it with himself. It was Rell, the person he had been waiting for, at least one of the people.

"Bruh, I been waiting on you for damn near 45 minutes," Damien said, both eyes closed once again. His body projecting a calm yet mildly irritated edge of impatience.

"My bad, that was very unprofessional of me huh?"

Before Damien could respond his rear passenger side door opened, and a very large man slid into the backseat.

"What up D?" said the large man.

"What up Jake!" Damien replied, reaching back with his right arm and bumping his fist against a large meaty knuckle. "Whatcha know good fool?"

"Man, trying to get like you."

Damien smiled and said, "Stop it." ending the ceremonial exchange of false flattery that occurred between two men of Damien and Jake's loose affiliation. They were friends; however, they were not… brothers. Still, Damien had always liked Jake, and they had known each other for quite some time, since grade school. Damien trusted Jake, and for tonight that was all that mattered. Damien looked over to the passenger seat to see Rell rifling through the contents of the backpack and then oddly to Damien's surprise, the driver's side rear door opened as well.

Damien's hand instinctively went to his lap, his fingers curled around the grip, his index finger brushing the trigger, the heavy metal gun bumped against his belt buckle and the hardly audible, but decisive 'pink' along with Damien's sudden jump made Rell look up from his rifling.

"Whoa-whoa, chill bro it's just Du-Whop," Rell said.

A fourth body slid itself into Damien's car.

"What up D?"

"Du-Whop!" Damien exclaimed, completely ignoring the newest passenger's greeting. "What the fuck is Du-Whop doing here?" Damien jerked and turned hard to look in the face of the person sitting behind him. Du-Whop smiled. Damien frowned and looked over at the passenger seat for his answer.

"What?" Said Rell, shrugging his shoulders and lifting his arm in surprise, both hands filled with wads of the rolled-up cash. "I figured we needed a taste tester and we could use the extra body."

"Are you fucking kidding me right now?"

"What?! It's Du-Whop, you know Du-Whop. Jake know Du-Whop, he was the safest bet."

The car was covered in a fog, what started out as a calm nervous anxiety had quickly turned to a thick hot tension.

"Are you stupid?" Damien asked.

"Fucker, are you gon snort a line pure uncut cocaine and tell us if it meets your highly discerning taste or not."

Damien was quiet, he looked forward.

"Thought so." Said Rell "Du-Whop is cool man, he gon do this shit with us make him a lil bit of money and we all gon walk away happy. Ain't that right Du-Whop?"

"That's the plan," Du-Whop said and then made a short quick sniffing sound that only served to irritate Damien further. "Aye yo D, I know it was last minute, but Rell said you would be cool with-it man. I'm only here to help baby, whatever you say to do, I do."

"This dude done brought a fucking junkie to a drug transaction, what the fuck?" Damien mumbled to himself, still ignoring Du-Whop in full.

"Bruh, relax its Du-Whop he's practically like an uncle to everybody in the hood anyway. It'll be fine."

"He ain't my fucking uncle. And don't tell me to relax." Damien turned back to Du-Whop addressing him for the first time since he entered the car. "Du-Whop I'm so serious right now, do not say or do any extra anything or I swear to God…"

"I gotcha D, I gotcha. I know this is your money on the line out here man, I'd never jeopardize that, come on now, you know me, baby."

"No, this is my life on the line. These dudes are a real deal drug cartel, they won't hesitate to kill me, you, or anybody else. I don't need any unpredictable type of shit around me tonight."

"Aye Du-Whop listen to Damien bruh, he already almost shot ya ass when we were getting in the car." Rell laughed as he spoke, placing the rolled-up wads of money back into the backpack. "He on edge tonight fool. Aye Jake, you got that other bag bruh?"

Jake handed Rell a brown paper bag over the seat. Rell took it and emptied the contents into Damien's open backpack. More rolled up wads of twenty-dollar bills spilled out of one bag and into the other.

"I got the other twenty-five thousand dollars here Mr. Damien Sills Jr. Sir." Rell said mockingly. Damien ignored him. "So that's seventy-fi-"

"Hold on." Damien interrupted. "Du-Whop, get out and look for these dudes to pull up. Knock on the window when you see'em coming."

"Fasho big dog, fasho," Du-Whop replied hoping out of the car with the enthusiasm of a summer intern.

Damien did not like Du-Whop. Not at the moment at least. Du-Whop was a drug addict, a dope head, a junkie. Crack cocaine was his drug of choice, but the old man was known to get high on whatever he could get his hands on. Rumor had it, Du-Whop, whose real name was Lou Olds, used to be quite the drug dealer himself, not much unlike Damien and Rell. He was a big and ambitious up-and-comer in New Hampton's emerging drug culture, and he had gotten the name Du-Whop from a magnanimous sense of style that made him look like a 1950's doo-wop singer. His hair pressed into a pompadour, his brightly colored suits, a large warm smile and a wide range of access to any number of recreational drugs made Lou Olds the life of every party in the New Hampton ghettos and within the cities elite social circles, but somewhere along the line, by some cruel twist of fate he had become the very thing upon which he preyed.

Du-Whop went from a seller to a user, to abuser, and before he knew it, he was buying hits from a couple of 14-year-old boys who were pushing their way into a business that had become much more ruthless and dangerous than the one that had destroyed his own life. Initially, he saw himself as a kind of a mentor to these young brothers, he would lecture them, telling them the ends and outs of the drug business during their transactions of him buying crack scores, pill hits and his bags and blunts of weed. At first, they seemed to listen, the would marvel at the stories of his glory days and laugh as he broke down the dance moves that guaranteed him a night with the woman or in some cases women of his choice. But over time Du-Whop began to suspect that the young brothers were not laughing with him nor were they in awe of his past feats, they were laughing at him. He was the drunken old fool that would dance and sing for their amusement. His stories and lessons were the ramblings of a broken old man that life had crushed under the heel of its boot. They cared for his messages, as about as much, as they cared for the message in a dog's bark. Their laughs and their eyes and their hearts were cold, and Du-Whop knew that they were better suited for the world of crime then he had ever been. For where he saw joy and mirth and merriment, they saw nothing but pain and anger. Ten years passed as Du-Whop watched Damien and Rell grow from boys to men and every year he took note as to how they seemed to grow darker and more heartless to the world around them, and though he told himself they were good boys on the inside, he slowly began to fear them. Their youth, ambition, and anger were menacing, like a hungry beast eager to consume, and like an old lion making way for the younger and more aggressive lions to lead, Du-Whop submitted himself to the young drug dealers, he was a forgotten king, and the laws of nature had conquered him in full.

Damien was afraid of Du-Whop, not in the traditional sense of fear, but in a way that not even Damien fully understood. For Damien, Du-Whop represented failure, weakness, a complete lack of self-discipline. Du-Whop had been, or had, at some point, the potential to be, somebody important. However, like a fool, he chose self-indulgence and the trifles of petty pleasures over business and look where that had gotten him. To Damien Du-Whop wasn't even a man anymore; he was a zombie, a husk, a shell of what used to be a man. He wandered around the

neighborhood, high and strung out, telling stories of what used to
be, singing and dancing for the dealers in the hopes that he might
get a slightly bigger rock, or a little bit more dope. Damien pitied
Du-Whop, and in the furnace of Damien's soul that pity turned
to resentment and the resentment manifested as anger and
disdain, but beneath it all, there was truly only fear. Above all else
in the world, Damien feared becoming Du-Whop.

The car door slammed shut with a defining thud.

"Alright," Damien looked back from the closing door and
over to Rell. "Talk."

Rell shook his head with a smile. "You're making him stand
outside."

Jake laughed from the backseat.

"He's on lookout," Damien said with a straight face. "And I'm
not about to talk dope with a junkie in the car, the whole
neighborhood will know our business before the weekend is
over."

Rell shrugged. "We got seventy-five thousand dollars, that's
going to buy us three kilograms of cocaine. The normal going
rate for a brick is thirty-four, we're getting them for twenty-five.
If we break down these bricks like we supposed to, we can make
fifty-seven thousand dollars, per kilo." Rell looked at Damien
with a very large grin. "Once we get this work, we looking to
make one hundred and seventy thousand dollars.

And that's just to start. We burn through these three bricks,
and we can get a lot more. We can see a million dollars inside of a
year."

"Now that's what the fuck I'm talking about," Jake said with a
clap.

"But it starts tonight," Damien said with a stern voice. "We get these three keys from Hector. We get them off fast, we show his organization that we can handle more."

"We'll be the kings of New Hampton by the summertime." Rell fist bumped Jake, who was glad to oblige.

"Bruh," Jake spoke up "Y'all put up the money, and I appreciate y'all bringing me in on this, so whatever ya need done." Jake flicked a meaty finger across his neck. "It's done."

"Speaking of." Rell turned in his seat. "Let me get that strap from back there." Jake handed Rell a 9mm handgun, and kept another gun, a large chrome one, for himself.

"D you still got that snub nose."

"Glove compartment."

Rell opened the glove box and pulled out a small snub nose revolver. He flicked open the chamber to find the gun fully loaded. He snapped it shut and handed it to Jake.

"Give that to Du-Whop."

Damien looked up as if he had something to say but held his silence. He looked back at Jake.

"Jake, I'm gonna be straightforward, you are the muscle. From this moment forward if anybody crosses the team, we need you to put the fear of God in 'em."

"I'm bringing down the hammer D, no questions asked."

"Now I don't expect any trouble tonight, but if this goes bad, then we have to wipe these guys out, get those bricks and prepare for war."

"Hector is normally cool, but D is right, these dudes can flip at any time. If you get the signal, shoot first ask questions later. Worst case we get the dope and keep all the money."

"No, worst case, we all end up dead, best case, we buy the dope, and we go back home; we get paid. Let's try and avoid anybody dying tonight."

"It's however you want to do it. Give the word, and I put bullets in heads." Jake said with cold finality.

At that moment Du-Whop knocked on the back window.

"They're here. Let's get this done." Said Damien.

Without hesitation, Jake hopped out of the car and joined Du-Whop outside. He passed Lou Olds Damien's revolver inconspicuously, and Du-Whop quickly jammed it into the waist of his pants. Inside the car, Damien turned to get out as well but felt an arm grip his elbow.

"Brother, it's been ten years we been out here in these streets." Rell had his signature grin painted across his face, "This has been a long time coming."

"It has but at the same time, nothing has changed, like I told you, a year from now I'm leaving New Hampton and all this shit far behind."

"Yeah yeah, keep telling yourself that, but when this money starts coming in you ain't gonna want to go nowhere."

"Ain't no retirement plan for a dope boy," Damien replied with a grin of his own. "unless you count the penitentiary, and I don't. I'm gonna turn my fifty thousand to half a million and then you and Jake can have it all."

"24 years old, talking about he retiring."

"You can come with me bruh."

"Man I been a hustler so long I wouldn't even know what to do with myself in... Where did you say you were going?"

"Ghana, I'm going to Ghana."

"I wouldn't know what to do with myself in Ghana fool."

"We'll think of something for you. Come on man lets handle this."

Damien and Rell exited the vehicle, with the backpack slung casually around Damien's shoulder. A large black SUV parked behind Damien's car and in front of the old sewing machine factory. Damien stepped forward, Rell closely behind him. Four fairly large men and one average sized man poured out of the SUV and into the abandoned lot.

"Karell Sanders!" Said the averaged sized man, his voice was boisterous and full of enthusiasm. "Hello, my friend. Sorry that we are late."

"Hector, mi amigo. It's all good. Your timing is perfect."

Hector smiled a huge, slightly menacing smile. Damien shrugged it off. Hector was Rell's contact, they had worked with him before, but it had always been through the filter of Rell's older cousin. Well now Rell's cousin was in prison, and Hector's organization was in need of a new contact in New Hampton, an ideal opportunity for ambitious young criminals. Coincidentally ideal opportunities made Damien very suspicious. It was not as if they hadn't earned it, according to Rell, at least. For the past ten years, they had scrambled hand to mouth trying to build a better life for themselves. Nickel and diming their way through the drug business, selling everything from weed to crack to heroin, anything they could buy cheap enough to make a profit from. When they couldn't afford to buy drugs cheap, then they'd steal them from rival dealers. This, of course, created friction, enemies, but Damien was smart, and Rell was ruthless, and this combination had kept them alive and out of prison for quite some time, and now it was offering new and exciting opportunities.

Hector smiled with an abnormally wide grin. He stood directly in front of the SUV. A large mass of muscle, in the shape of a man, stood on either side of him, two more stood in the back. He had four henchmen, each roughly the size of Jake, if not larger.

"Damien." Said Hector, looking at Damien with hungry eyes. Purely out of instinct, Damien almost reached for his gun, but instead only responded with a weary hello.

"Hector. Thank you for meeting with us, we really appreciate -"

"Ah Damien, always business. Black Frank was right about you." Hector cut Damien off mid-sentence.

"Black Frank?" Damien was confused. Frank was Rell's cousin.

"Yes, he says that you are a very shrewd businessman. He says that you have… potential." With this last statement, Hector seemed almost to let out a laugh, as did the large men that accompanied him. Damien felt as if he were the butt end of an inside joke, and noted, distinctly, that he did not like it. "Who else is this you all have with you?"

Rell spoke up, "This is our man Jake, and this is Du-Whop."

"I see." Hector eyed Jake and Du-Whop with passive unconcerned glances. "To business then." Hector snapped his fingers and lifted an open hand. On command one of the large men handed him a small duffle bag. "Five Kilos," Hector said extending his arm and therefore the duffel bag full cocaine towards Damien and Rell.

"Umm Hector, we only agreed to three kilos. We didn't bring enough money for-"

Hector cut Rell off mid-speech the same was he did Damien.

"Consider it a gift, an act of good faith in the spirit of our new partnership."

Five kilos, with a street value of fifty-seven thousand dollars per kilo, that's a seventy-five thousand dollar investment that'll turn a profit of two hundred and ten thousand dollars. Two hundred and ten thousand dollars. TWO HUNDRED AND TEN THOUSAND DOLLARS. It had taken Damien ten years to scrape up fifty thousand dollars, and now within 3 maybe 4 months, he was going to be holding two hundred and ten thousand dollars.

"Is this a loan?" Damien asked. "Are the extra kilos on credit?"

Hector smiled his hungry-eyed smile. "Ah Damien, no my friend, it is not a loan. They are yours. No strings attached."

Damien removed the backpack from his shoulder and offered it to Hector, another of the large men quickly came forward and grabbed the bag from Damien's hand.

"Its seventy-five thousand dollars, you can count it…" Damien began.

"There is no need," said Hector. "I trust you."

Hector's arm bobbed, the cocaine duffle bag still in his extended hand. Rell moved forward reluctantly and took hold of the satchel like a cautious animal eating from the hand of an unfamiliar human caretaker. Hector released the bag but never took his eyes off of Damien. Not even for a moment.

Before Rell could step back from Hector, the same henchman that handed his boss the satchel of cocaine at the snap of a finger, flicked out an indecently large switchblade seemingly without warning. Every member of Damien's party jumped, moving toward, however not fully reaching for, their respective firearms. Once again Hector's gang seemed to giggle under their breath. Damien was beginning to feel like he and his crew were in some type of drug dealer amateur hour and at that moment, more so then any moment before, Damien wanted to complete and escape this transaction as quickly as possible.

"For you," Hector said gesturing to the knife all while still maintaining his ever-present eye contact. "To sample the product."

"We trust you," Damien replied. And with this Hector and each of his mean erupted in laughter, so much so that Hector eyes closed, and his head flew back finally ending the stare down between him and Damien in a way that Damien felt he could at least feel dignified about.

"I insist," said Hector with a straight face, and immediately Damien knew that he was not being given an option. With each passing second, the encounter was feeling less like a drug transaction, and more and more like a game of cat and mouse and Damien could feel that cat's hot breathe upon his face.

"Du-Whop." Damien motioned the old man forward.

Du-Whop shambled to center stage and with a nod took the switchblade from Hector's more active goon. Rell held the cocaine satchel open, and Du-Whop peered inside like a child peers inside a trick or treating bucket on Halloween. Not necessarily in salivating anticipation, but rather in the intimidating awe of being given enormous quantities of candy from strangers for doing nothing more than having the balls to show up at their doorstep. Du-Whop stuck his hand into the duffle bag and pulled out a tightly wrapped brick of cocaine. He used the knife to make a slit in the packaging and pulled the knife out balancing a small lump of flaky white powder on the blade. There was one quick, strong snort, and instantly his sinus cavity burned as if he had just sniffed hellfire. He winced and threw his head back. Closed eyes squeezed out tears that rolled down the side of each cheek. Du-Whop felt a flash behind his eyes and felt the sensation of fireworks going off inside his brain. Tiny explosions of euphoria ignited here and there in random succession. His face went numb.

"Product's good," Du-Whop grunted, and with a sniffling swipe of his nose, he placed the cocaine back into the bag before slapping Rell on the shoulder and going back to his previous post on the outskirts of the conversation. His head still swimming from the effects of the drug.

Hector laughed out loud once again. "I really like you guys; you really know how to do business."

Rell dropped down to one knee and began to zip the duffle bag closed. Time to go, Damien thought. This deal is done. We can get out of here now before anything goes wrong. They have the money we have the dope everything is goo—

"One more thing." Hector said with a smile, "Damien. My employer is always in need of new young talent and we um, we think you fit the bill."

Damien's mind twisted. What was he talking about?

"We'd like you to come work for us."

"Work for you?"

"Yes, our organization could use a man like you."

"I don't understand."

"What is there to understand, we want you to come with us. It's quite simple my friend."

"Now?" Damien asked, confused, surprised and becoming very very anxious.

"Right now." Said Hector with no hesitation.

Rell stood up immediately, he looked just as bewildered as Damien was. They read the confusion on each other's face. This was going all wrong.

"Hector, mi compadre, thanks for the offer but I don't think we are really interested in any full-time positions, at least not right now I mean. Maybe once we get this—"

Hector silenced Rell with a single raised hand. He pointed, and the goon holding the backpack full of money threw it into Rell's arms.

Mr. Sanders, we have no interest in you. We only want Damien. You can have your money back, you can keep the drugs, and you can get out of here. Damien, we would like you, to come with us."

Damien dared not take his eyes off of Hector, but from the side of his vision, he could see Rell's movements and even before

Rell moved a muscle, Damien knew where this was heading. Karell did not respond well to intimidation.

Rell dropped the bag of cocaine behind him and almost as if on cue Jake picked it up and handed it off to Du-Whop. Rell put the backpack on, a strap over each shoulder, and then he pulled the 9mm handgun from the small of his back.

"My brother is not for sale. And I don't know where you think you are, but in New Hampton, we don't turn our back on our own. So, we will take *our* money, and we will take *your* drugs, and you can take yo ass and get the fuck outta here. Your night is done."

Damien saw Jake pull his gun as well. He put his hand under his shirt, palming the grip of his own piece. This was really about to happen.

Hector let out a sigh. "Ahhh Mr. Sanders, your tenacity is almost admirable." Hector looked at one of his henchmen. "Kill him."

The man closest to Hector's left began to walk toward Rell with a smirk across his face. Rell raised his gun.

"My man, if you take another step I'm going to shoot that ugly ass smile right off of your face," Rell said, his gun drawn and being held with both hands. At his current range, it would have been impossible for him to miss. Damien was left with no other choice; he pulled his gun too. He held it with both hands, still pointed at the ground, ready to turn it on any of the other henchmen or even Hector himself if need be. Damien had never shot anyone, and definitely not this close before. He hated the idea of the first person he shot and killed being a member of a drug cartel, but as things appeared, he would not have many options.

The henchman turned his glance back to Hector who gave him an approving nod to continue his march.

"I said DON'T MOVE!"

The goon took another step.

There was a loud pop, pop, pop in quick succession. Damien heard the shell casing make a melodic bell-like sound as they bounced onto the worn concrete asphalt of the abandoned parking lot. Rell had pulled the trigger. Three shots had hit the advancing henchmen square in the chest. The man stood frozen, his head slumped over and his right hand clenching his wounded chest. He teetered as if he was about to fall forward but then slowly leaned back into his standing position. His right hand dropped to his side; it was covered in blood that dripped from his fingertips. He stood in perfect stillness for what must have been three whole seconds, an impossibly long time to have taken three gunshot wounds to the chest. For a moment Damien had thought the man had died on his feet, but then he heard it, a terrible unnerving sound that made his soul shudder upon impact. It was laughing. The man was laughing. The wounded man, bleeding from the chest, shot at damn near point blank range, was laughing. It was a heady and robust laugh as if he had been holding it in all night. And as he began, the other started laughing too. As if being shot in the chest was some type of hilariously sick joke. Damien looked up at Hector who was not laughing but who was grinning. That hungry-eyed, wide mouth grin and he was pointing it directly at Damien.

Damien raised his gun, shakily aiming for Hector.

"What is this, what the fuck is going on?"

"Ahhh Damien, " Hector ran his fingers through his slick black hair, and as he spoke the laughs begin to turn to growls "It is simple… For we wrestle not against flesh and blood," Hector twitched, "but against principalities, against powers," His face contorted in pain, "against the rulers of the darkness of this world." Hector seemed to be growing taller "against spiritual wickedness in HIGH PLACES."

Hector's voice changed as it tapered off on his final words. It had become deeper and more splintered, almost as if he was clearing his throat while talking. His neck twisted and for some reason, Damien could hear bones cracking, breaking and resetting themselves. Hector's face began to change, his cheekbones popped, caved into his face and then violently jutted forward, dragging his top jaw and nose along with it. Teeth, at first perfect and white, grew jagged, long and menacingly sharper, his hair started to turn a dark shade of brown and sprouted from every exposed pore on his body, his face, neck, and arms begin to vanish underneath a mat of this dark amber colored fur. Damien froze. He couldn't wrap his mind around what his eyes were seeing. Hector was changing; getting bigger, wider, taller. His clothes begin to rip and tear as they grew too small for his frame. He was turning into a monster, astounding and terrifying. He now stood at over seven feet, covered in fur and still staring out of those same hungry eyes. His arms and legs were as thick as tree limbs, all tightly wrapped in lean muscle. His mouth had been replaced with a muzzle; black lips curled back, and a sickening white foam oozed through the spacing of new teeth. Teeth made for tearing and ripping.

"Are you fucking shitting me?" Damien mumbled, not even fully aware that he was speaking.

The monster looked down at him with something that resembled a smile. "I shit you not." It replied in a voice that in no way could be mistaken for human. It let out a terrible laugh.

Damien heard more gunshots. He looked to Rell to see another beastman walking toward him, this one black and advancing in slow, methodical steps. Rell was unloading round after round into the thing's chest. It didn't seem to notice in the slightest. With a powerful swipe of its huge paw, the monster slapped Rell's gun from his hand. Damien's friend let out a yelp of pain and grabbed for his wrist, but before he could even stumble backward, the animal grabbed him by the throat lifting him off the ground like he was stuffed with hay as opposed to flesh and bones.

"Nooooo!" Damien advanced toward the monster firing his weapon with every step. The gun barked and spat fire at the command of the trigger. It bucked under the force of the exploding barrel, and Damien's shot flew rapidly and with vicious momentum but with no concentrated accuracy. Bullets whizzed pass the monster, miss after miss. One hit, pelting the beast in the arm. It was ignored just as the others to the chest were, and then, one skitted past its muzzle, only grazing it, but finally getting its attention. The thing's head turned toward Damien, and in a motion, it slammed Rell's body into the concrete and then placed a paw-like foot on the crumpled heap. It snarled in Damien's direction, its ears rolled back and its teeth fully bared, it was a challenge.

Damien began to run towards the thing, challenge accepted, he didn't know what he would do, he didn't know how to fight this thing that absorbed bullets, but he had to do –

Damien was hit hard from his left side, his body hit the ground, and an immovable weigh kept him pinned to it. He had been tackled, snatched out of the air mid-stride and slammed onto his back. The animal-like thing that use to be Hector was on top of him, its gargantuan body pressed down upon Damien's chest. He was trapped and getting up an impossibility. Somehow between being swept off of his feet and put on to his back

Damien had managed to get his elbow and forearm between himself and the animal's throat, it was by this stroke of luck alone that auburn beast that use to be Hector was not currently eating Damien's face. The thing snapped and snarled dripping foam and salvia onto Damien's forehead as it tried quite tenaciously to get Damien's skull within reach of its jaws. Its large long mouth slammed repeatedly shut inches from Damien's nose. It's hot breath stank of blood and raw meat and the only thing keeping Damien alive was the desperation laced strength he managed to muster and maintain to keep this savage and feral creature from getting any closer. He pushed with everything he had and knew immediately that it was not enough. His strength waned, and all his life's aspiration and dreams were reduced to just hoping to stay alive for a few more seconds. Damien continued to push, an action that he was so preoccupied with, that he hadn't noticed that as he lay under the monstrous creature that he had begun to scream. A scream not born of fear or panic but of something much more instinctual. The scream was raucous and visceral, it was more of a reaction than an intention. It was the sound that escaped desperate men in a last-ditch, adrenaline filled effort to prolong their lives, and by some miracle, it seemed to work. Damien felt the pressure and weight of Hector's bestial body lift from his chest. Slow and deliberate at first, as if was Damien was bench pressing the world, and then there was a fast and hard release of pressure, and with a violent jerk he was free. Damien scrambled to roll over and found himself on his hand and knees, his eyes darted in every direction, what had happened, how was he— and then he saw it. It was Jake. He had bum-rushed the transformed Hector performing a tackle of his own. Jake's massive size and his running start apparently gave him the momentum to topple the monster off of Damien, but now he was stuck in a wrestling match with the thing.

"Go D!" Jake screamed trying desperately to hold the thing down. It seemed to be still genuinely surprised by Jake's initial action, and that confusion was Jake's current advantage. "Get Rell out of here."

Jake still had his gun in his hand, he tried to bring it and place it directly against the creature's skull, but before he could do so, the thing that use to be Hector seemed to recover from his initial surprise and with a twist and slip freed itself from Jake's grasp and bit down hard on his arm. Damien swore that he could hear bones crunch as Jake screamed in agony. Even as Hector was freeing himself and preparing his counterattack, the other monsters had begun to converge on Jake at once. By the time of the bite, three other monsters were closing in on Jake and Hector with unnerving ferocity. A hand grabbed Damien shoulder, he spun with a jerk attempting to aim a gun that he no longer gripped in his hands. He looked to see Du-Whop standing over him, pulling him up to his feet.

"Let's grab Rell, we gotta get outta here!" Du-shop screamed over the growls and snarls. Damien followed Du-Whop a few yards over to where Rell lay. There was a large and lifeless fur-covered body lying next to his. It was one of the creatures, it was dead. "Jake shot it square in the head when it wasn't looking, when it was focused on you. It dropped like a ton of bricks." Du-Whop explained as if he heard the thoughts racing through Damien's head.

Damien looked back at Jake. Hector still had a mouth full of his arm and was now shaking his head viciously like a wild dog locking down on a piece of meat. The other creatures had reached them now, and Damien watched helplessly as each animal clamped on to a section of available flesh. Jake screamed out again. There were four of these massive nightmares on him. Hector on his left forearm another behind him biting into his right shoulder, the third latching on his right leg and the fourth clambered over the others desperate to sink its teeth into the side of Jake's rib cage. It was hopeless. There was no way for Jake to escape the four of them. Through sheer willpower Jake still gripped his gun, he forced his right arm to bend at the elbow and bring the barrel to the direction of his head. He was losing consciousness. Damien could see it, he took a step towards them but felt a hand grab his shirt to stop him from going any further. Jake had moved the gun closer to his head, it pointed straight into the air now, and due to the things constraining his movement it would go no further. Jake bent his arm hard at the wrist and with a final yell, Jake set the gun against the head of the monster gnawing at his shoulder and pulled the trigger. The chrome desert eagle erupted and launched a .50 caliber ammunition round directly through the skull of the beast. The thing released its grip and fell to the ground in a slump. The other creatures seemed unperturbed by this and continued their ferocious attack with impunity. Jake went limp, and his gun fell to the ground with the clatter of metal on concrete. Damien looked away as the beast men chewed on his friend's lifeless body.

Du-Whop was shaking Damien's shoulder hard. "Damien, we have to go, we gotta run."

Damien looked Du-Whop in the face, "Where's Rell?" he asked. The question vocalized far more calmly then he intended.

Du-Whop shook his head. "He's gon D, they killed him."

Damien looked pass Du-Whop and at the ground where Rell lay. What was happening? Rell was dead? Dead? And he was expected to leave him? To just leave his body lying there? With these, these… monsters?

Damien felt a cold sting bite him hard on the right cheek, and with the pain, the entire world around him came back into focus. Du-Whop had just slapped him. "Put this on." Du-Whop put Damien's arms through the loops of the backpack. "Now move it, we're gonna try and make a run for the church."

"But the car is right here." Damien protested, finally somewhat back in his right mind, or as right as present conditions would allow.

"Then go!" Du-Whop broke into a sprint and Damien followed closely behind him. They dashed toward the car hoping to dive in and peel off with their lives and limbs intact. Damien moved toward his own car and before he could reach the door handle a heavy body seemed to fall from the sky landing on the top of the car shattering the windows and caving in the roof. Damien looked up to see the beast form of Hector snarling down at him blood dripping from his maw, his huge fur covered body crushing Damien's car. Hector rose, standing to his full height atop the destroyed vehicle, the beast man leaned back, his snarl a primitive hybrid between a wolfish sneer and the same menacing grin Hector had paraded all evening. The beast took in a big breath and with the full moon shimmering behind him, released a blood-curdling howl that Damien felt ring deep in his chest. On cue, the other beast men took a momentary respite from their feeding and released howls in concert with Hector.

The howling crushed something inside Damien, he dropped down to one knee, his eyes shut tight and his hands covering his ears. He imagined he was feeling, at that moment, the way a rabbit felt when staring into the gaping jaws of a wolf preparing to devour it. Death is imminent, and life has no meaning. 24 years on the streets of New Hampton all to die in an alley ripped apart by a man-beast after a bad coke deal. If it wasn't so horrifically terrifying, it could almost be funny. Damien felt a sharp tug at this arm, and then heard the screaming of a familiar voice which sliced through the noise and confusion of Hector's howling.

"DAMIEN! MOVE!" Du-Whop screamed, pulling Damien's arm lifting him off of his knees and back onto his feet. With his other hand, Du-Whop squeezed the trigger on the snub-nosed revolver he had been given earlier. Three loud pops rang in

Damien's ears. The monster Hector took two bullets in the chest, and a third skidded across his beastly face.

Damien didn't give himself a chance to see the monster's reaction; he took Du-Whop's advice and immediately started running. His feet belted across the pavement carrying him towards the front side of the abandoned church building. He looked back only long enough to see Du-Whop was still behind him, gun in one hand and the drug-filled duffle bag still slung across his shoulder. Further behind Du-Whop, Damien heard yelling.

"Do you think you can run from me, Damien? Do you REALLY THINK YOU CAN ESCAPE!!!" It was the voice of a demon, deep and guttural, filled with more malice and rage then Damien had ever heard. His stomach turned, and he felt his knees wobble under him. He willed himself to run faster. He and Du-Whop made it to the front of the church and Damien instinctively reached out for the door, half expecting them to be locked but, in a life or death situation, the laws of self-preservation deemed it necessary to at least try. Much to Damien's surprise, the doors swung open.

"Du-Whop, inside!" Damien screamed over his shoulder. Du-Whop pushed his way inside the church, slamming the doors closed behind him. Damien reached down and grabbed a heavy iron candlestick holder knocked off the still burning candles and jammed it between the door handles.

"Here, help me put this in front of it." Du-Whop was attempting to lift a pew, Damien hoisted up the other end, and they managed to drag it in front of the door.

"Another," Damien said as they dropped the first one into place, and together the two heaved a second pew on top of the first thoroughly blocking the only entryway into the church.

Damien and Du-Whop slowly backed away from the doors, both of their eyes glued to the makeshift blockade, waiting intently for the banging and scratching to begin.

"Wha… what is going on?" Damien muttered, as if afraid to speak. "What are those things?"

"They're exactly what they look like D…." Du-Whop reached into his shirt pocket and pulled a cigarette from a half-empty pack. His hand shook with tremors of either an abundance of adrenaline or from a lack of a myriad of other drugs his body now felt were necessities for its proper function, Damien could not tell which, not that it mattered much at the moment. Damien looked down at his own hands, he was shaking as well. "They're werewolves… Lycanthropes." On the final word, Du-Whop's lighter struck perfect, lighting the end of his cigarette.

"Were-Werewolves, how is this? Why is this… they killed Jake, they killed Rell."

"No," Du-Whop cut in, "Rell is still alive."

"What!?"

"Rell isn't dead, He's hurt but not dead." Du-Whop took another drag of his cigarette, but before he could exhale the smoke, Damien had grabbed him by the collar of his cruddy green army jacket.

"Nigga you told me he was dead, I left him behind because you told me he was dead!"

"We had too" Du-Whop didn't bother trying to push Damien off of him. "His leg was crushed when that big wolf either slammed down or fell on him. I tried to get him up after Jake shot the damn thing. He couldn't move. I told him just to stay put, play dead. "

"Play dead? Are you crazy this ain't the fucking boy scouts those things ATE Jake, they'll…"

"The Wolves were after you D. They didn't want Rell. I told him I'd get you out of there and they'd follow us, and once he was sure they'd gone, he could get away. I told him to stay put and stay quiet. He's hurt, but he's alive."

"Well we have to go back out there, we gotta go get him." Damien released Du-Whop and began moving toward the door, but a surprisingly strong grip on his shoulder stopped him.

"That's not possible, we barely made it here alive, and we can't even be sure how long this will last. We have to get you out of here and to someplace safe."

"SAFE?! Fool there are fucking werewolves outside. Fucking man-eating werewolves… Wha-what in the hell happening??" Damien began to pace back and forth in the aisle between the pews.

"Damien, I know you're confused and I-"

"Confused!? I'm not confused I'm scared shitless, this… this is…"

"Kid listen, I know what you're going through, I can help you, I have answers, but you gotta calm down."

"Answers? You got answers? Yo, in case you ain't noticed, you'a fucking junkie Whop. A dope head, life in itself has proven that you ain't got NO fucking answers nigga, you ain't got shit. You probably still high on that coke you hit outside so what in the fuck could you possibly understand huh, what could you possibly tell me?" Even as Damien spoke the words, he immediately regretted them, from the moment things had begun to go awry Du-Whop had become inexplicably reliable. In fact,

the old man had saved his life at least three times already and had
he not been there Damien would have surely been dead long ago.
He didn't deserve to be talked to like this, but Damien was angry
and afraid, and since he had nowhere else to focus his fear and
rage, insults spewed from his mouth like angry word vomit. "D-
Du-Whop, I'm sorry man, I-I didn't mean that."

"It's fine." Du-Whop took another long drag of his cigarette.
"You know, I get it young blood. My time is over, been over for a
long time now, and you boys… you boys are the future. Ain't no
denying that. I know what y'all say about me, Old man Du-
Whop, crack fiend, sherm head, dancing for a hit, singing for a
joint. You think I don't know I'm the laughing stock of the south
side. But you check this here baby boy, everything ain't always
what it seems, and it's a lot more to this here world then what
you see on the surface."

"Noooooo." Damien threw his head back covering his face
with his hands. "This cannot be happening… Wait, that's it. This
can't be happening, it's impossible. I must be dreaming."

Damien took another step backward, stepping on something
and crushing it under the heel of his shoe, almost simultaneously
he heard a faint bang and a knock from the back of the church.
He spun around, eyes scanning the room. He made note of the
ornate carving of the wooden trim that decorated the raised dais
on which the pulpit stood. His eyes focused in on the doors at
the back of the room expecting at any moment for a fur-covered
man-beast to come rushing out. The moment passed, and no
beast came. Damien looked down at his feet and picked up the
broken candle he had stepped on by mistake. The candle was
long and white except for the smoldering blackened wick. At one
end of the candle, a thin wisp of smoke slipped from its
previously lit tip and dissipated into the nothing right before
Damien's eyes.

"Someone's here," Damien said aloud.

"What?" Du-Whop responded busy wrestling another cigarette from its pack and now struggling to light it.

"I thought this place was abandoned, but there's someone here. These candles were lit when we came in, and I think I just heard someone."

Du-Whop lifted his head with a newly lit cigarette between his lips. He allowed his eyes to quickly survey the interior of the cathedral. The inside of what should have been a broken down and dilapidated building, filled with cobwebs, shattered windows and random graffiti was instead immaculately clean and well kept. The church's high ceilings, stained glass windows, and brass chandeliers all sparkled under a layer of freshly applied polish. Heavy wooden pews filled the room, organized in tight, precise rows facing and leading up to a largely raised pulpit which sat on the far end of the room. The Pulpit jutted out from the back wall of the cathedral with large ornate doors positioned on either side offset by confessional booths.

"I'm more worried about the things on the outside than any person on the inside," Du-Whop said, but as he spoke, he began to slowly walk toward the far end of the church, making his way closer and closer to the pulpit and the doors that sat to either side of it. Damien looked back at the blocked door and began to follow Du-Whop through the church. Realizing that he had lost his gun, Damien reached down and picked up a heavy silver looking candlestick holder. He gripped and re-gripped it in his right hand, attempting to quickly become used to its weight and convincing himself it would make a good weapon against things that were unfazed by bullets.

By now Du-Whop was halfway to the back of the church and before he could take another step the large ornate doors to the left of the pulpit swung open.

"I'll tolerate no thieves or vandals in this house of the Lord, drop you're weapons or so help me God I'll send ye all to meet yer maker right bloody now!"

From between the ornate doors stepped a priest, dressed in black and wearing the signature white collar, only this priest was moving fast and aggressively and holding in his hands the biggest shotgun Damien had ever seen. The priest had the barrel of the gun pointed directly at him and Du-Whop, and from the way, the man moved he seemed surprisingly comfortable and assumingly proficient with the weapon. Damien instinctively rose his candlestick holder in defense, and for a moment he thought of throwing it at the man in the hopes of either distracting or disarming the holy gunman, at least long enough to give him and Du-Whop some sort of edge over the extremely deadly looking shotgun. At the same time, Du-Whop had raised his gun. He was still holding the snub-nosed revolver that Jake had given him earlier, and if Damien remembered correctly, he still had at least three shots in it.

"Whoa whoa whoa!" Du-Whop screamed out. "We're not thieves, we need help."

"Not thieves, well aren't you holding a gun, haven't you already ransacked the front of my church and isn't your bloody accomplice holding one of my candlestick holders!"

Du-Whop looked back to see Damien standing with the raised candlestick holder "Put that down D…."

"What?" Damien responded, "He's holding a shotgun."

"Exactly, what is that candlestick holder gonna do against a shotgun. Just put it down."

Damien acquiesced and lowered the candlestick holder down to his side but did not drop it. Du Whop turned back to the priest and placed his own hands in the air, leaving the revolver dangling from his finger.

"See," Du-Whop said calmly, "We don't want any trouble, we just need some help."

There was a familiar sound of mechanical parts moving, only much louder and much more menacing than it had been when Damien had made the sound himself earlier. The Priest had cocked the shotgun.

"Start talking laddie."

At the sound of the shotgun cocking Damien's heart dropped, he should have thrown the damned candlestick holder when he had the chance. Now they were dead for sure. From killer werewolves to a killer priest. Out of the frying pan and into the fire.

"My man, hold on one minute if you'll just listen to me, outside there are these things-"

"Hold on a bloody second…. Lou? Lou Olds is that you."

Du-Whop paused in the middle of his explanation, and for a moment he seemed confused, and then,

"Art?" Du-Whop's head turned in the way that heads do when the mind starts making a connection that it previously thought impossible. "Arthur Bright"

At that, the priest lowered the shotgun and then moved in with the same speed and aggressiveness and threw his free arm around Du-Whop. The two men hugged like old friends reuniting under the oddest of circumstances. The priest let Du-Whop go only to reach back out and grab hold to his head and neck.

"Bloody hell mate, I thought you were dead! Where have you been all these years and what in God's name have ye been doing?" It was only now that the threat of immediate death had waned did Damien notice how strong the priest accent was, Irish, or Scottish he assumed, but in actuality had no way of knowing.

"I've been here in New Hampton for the past 10 years, living off the grid... under the radar."

"Jesus mate, you barely look like yourself, I almost blasted you into next Sunday!"

"Nevermind me, what are you doing here?" Du-Whop asked the priest.

"Charles sent me here a couple of years ago, I'm supposed to be watching the area, keeping an eye out for threats and potentials and the like."

Du-Whop sniffed, looked back at Damien and then looked back at the priest, "Well looks like today is your lucky day."

Part II

"Does anybody wanna tell me what's going on?" Damien asked, the candlestick holder still in his hand.

"Who's the boy?" the priest asked Du-Whop, completely ignoring Damien's question.

"He's my tyro, stumbled upon him and another boy back in my old neighborhood, been watching over them since I got back."

"And did you find them the same way Charles found you?"

"Pretty much," Du-Whop answered, "They were on a less than desirable path, but I think this one had the right of it, was looking to make his escape, but they found him first."

"What's the situation?"

"Lycanthropes, Strykers, all very strong."

"Shite… and what do they want?"

"They're after the boy, they hurt one of his friends pretty bad, killed another… but not before he managed to kill two of them."

"He must have been one tough bastard."

"He was a good kid, just happen to be at the wrong place at the wrong time." Du-Whop paused for a moment. "There are still three left."

"What do you want to do?"

"I can't let them have the boy, I have to get him out of here… no matter the cost." Du-Whop looked back at Damien once again. Damien was looking back at him, his eyebrows raised in both frustration and confusion.

"Are you ready to tell me what the hell you two are talking about? Why are werewolves outside and why are they after me? And more importantly, how are we going to get past them, grab Rell and get out of here without them eating us."

"Lou, I thought you said this was your tyro? He's bloody clueless!" the priest remarked.

"He is," Du-Whop responded, "But it has not been the typical relationship."

"What the hell is a tyro?" Damien asked getting more and more frustrated with the lack of answers he was receiving.

"A Tyro is like a student or a pupil, but often times, as obviously in your case it means Lou here has been playing the role of your guardian angel. Protecting you and watching your back and judging by the number of Lycanthropes on yer arse you've been lucky to have him up to this point."

"Guardian angel? Du-Whop?" He's not…" Damien was about to continue, but thought better of it; instead, he looked to Du-Whop. "Whop what's going on man?"

Du-Whop sat down and let out a long and heavy sigh, then reached in his pocket for another cigarette.

"There are Werewolves outside right? But see, they're not like they are in the movies. They can change back and forth whenever they want, they're smart, and they are more than ruthless. One of them still has the ability to talk, even when he is transformed. That means he's old… strong."

Du-Whop took a drag of what Damien took note to be at least his third cigarette, as he exhaled the cigarette smoke, Damien couldn't help but breath it in and as he did he could feel the second-hand smoke work its calming magic on his fried nerve endings, suddenly he understood why nicotine could seem so appealing. He then also realized what horrible shape he was in. His throat locked up, making it nearly impossible to swallow, his body ached all over, and a cold, wet, sticky feeling followed by sharp stinging pain on his elbow, knees and the left side of his rib cage let him know that he was bleeding, more than likely from scrapes incurred in his scuffle with Hector. He had half a mind to bum a cigarette from Du-Whop, and then remembered that he didn't smoke cigarettes.

"They're tough too. Unlike the movies they don't give a shit about silver and guns like these won't even slow them down" Du-Whop held up his small revolver. Well, it was actually Damien's revolver. A .38, snub nose Smith & Wesson, Model 64 to be exact. Stainless steel with a woodgrain handle. It was ugly and stumpy and just so happened to be Damien's first and therefore favorite gun, and according to Du-Whop, it was useless. "It's not strong enough to do any real damage to those things, the only way to kill a werewolf is to destroy the brain, and a .38 is not strong enough to penetrate the skull. You'd need something bigger .50 caliber at least, and even then, you'd need to be close, very close. Like your friend…. Jake."

Damien stood solemnly at the mention of Jake's name and quietly hoped that what had happened to him was not currently happening to Rell. He couldn't bear the thought.

"I don't have a .50 Cal, but I do have this." Said the priest. Holding up the shotgun, "And Lizzie here has enough stopping power to flatten a charging grizzly. She'll make short work of any one of those slobbering bastards that gets to close."

"Thanks, Art, but I can't ask you to do that."

"Ask me hell, this is my job! It's why I'm here!"

"Thanks my man…" said Du-Whop but still with a look of regret in his eyes.

"Wait wait, hold on a minute, what do you mean it's your job? And Du-Whop how in the hell do you know all this shit about werewolves."

"Jesus Laddie, watch your language, have some respect for this holy place ye little bastard!"

Damien cut his eyes at the priest, who had used more foul language then either he or Du-Whop combined.

"Damien, this is Arthur Bright, priest and former colleague of mine."

"Yeah, nice to meet you Reverend," Damien said dismissively. "Whop, how in the hell are you a Werewolf expert?"

"I started off in New Hampton like you, hustling, dealing. Along the way, I got into the wrong side of it with some very bad guys. Thought I had it all under control, but I was in much deeper than I knew. Then someone stepped in and helped me, offered me a way out."

"You mean like as in an informant?" Even with the threat of being eaten by werewolves looming overhead, Damien cringed at the thought of Du-Whop being a confidential informant… a snitch.

"No." Du-Whop scoffed. "This was a little bit bigger than government agents and jail time. Hell, I would have given my left arm to go to prison. But no, I wasn't an informant. I was someone with potential, and the people I was dealing with then, just like the people we are dealing with now, they really like people with potential."

"What does that mean 'Potential' everyone has potential, that doesn't explain why Werewolves are trying to eat me!"

"They are not trying to eat you; they are trying to turn you!"

"What?" Damien now felt even more confused.

"If they wanted you dead, they would have killed you already. They want to make you one of them."

"Wh-why me?"

"Not everyone can survive being afflicted with Lycanthropy, if the average person is bitten by a werewolf they just die, painfully and horribly, but then there are a few people have the propensity to survive the conversion. And that's who these people are looking for. I don't know how else to explain it other than to just say that you have something that most people don't. There is something inside you, an energy, or a power, something imperceptible, but there. Whatever it is, these people can sense it, they can smell it, and they want it..." He took another long drag from his cigarette, "baby boy they want it bad."

"Du-Whop what the hell are you talking about?" Damien's voice cracked under the strain of stress and desperation. "Ain't nothing special about me. I'm a drug dealer. You're a drug addict, and outside there are werewolves… WEREWOLVES! Let's forget about the fairy tales and deal with the issue at hand. We need to get Rell and get out of here?"

"Drug Addict?!" Said Art from the left of the conversation. "So that's it yeah? You've been using those drugs to hide, burying yourself and your spirit energy underneath a smog. It's no wonder I didn't notice you sitting here right under my nose."

Du-Whop took another hit of his cigarette, he didn't bother responding or even looking at Art as he spoke.

There was a bang, hard and loud, almost as if a medieval battering ram had been slammed against the large wooden doors of the church entrance. All three men turned toward the source of the noise, frozen in a sudden panic. There was another bang, this one just as loud as the first. Damien could have sworn he felt the entire church building shudder, and the slight tingling of chandelier crystals overhead let him know that it was not completely his imagination. A third bang, and this time there was no question as to if the building shook or not. This time every lit candle in the church flickered as if blown upon by a gentle wind while at the same time dust fell from the rafters, knocked loose by the same force that Damien could feel reverberating through him like the bass line from his car radio speakers used too.

"Little pig, little pig, let me in…" A grizzled and growling voice cut through the walls of the church building and hit Damien in the chest like a bullet, his stomach folded in upon itself and for a moment he thought he might throw up. It was Hector, speaking in his wolf form, it was unmistakable, and for the first time since entering the church, Damien was reminded of how terrified he really was.

"They're here!" Damien said without really trying to speak.

Du-Whop stood to his feet; the cigarette dropping from his lips and extinguishing itself on the church floor. Art pointed the shotgun barrel toward the church doors, not really aiming but more so, subconsciously placing the business end of the shotgun between himself and the thing on the other side of the doors.

"Art, does this place have a back door? This may be our only chance. We can sneak out of the back and grab Rell in the process if we're lucky we'll only have one wolf to fight off." Du-Whop ran through his plan quickly, the entire time his voice calm and steady. The term 'Grace under fire' popped into Damien's mind.

"Yes, we can cut through my office and – "

"Little piggies! I have one of your friends out here, shall I make him squeal to prove it?"

There was a brief moment of silence, and then there was a scream, a human scream, loud and full of agony and to Damien, very very distinct. Damien's eyes grew wide, it was unmistakable.

"It's Rell! HE HAS RELL!"

"Daaaaaaaamien," Hector taunted." I have your friend, and if you do not come out of that church, I'll rip his throat out!"

Without a word, Damien began quickly making his way to the church doors. Before he got too far a sturdy hand gripped his shoulder.

"Damien you cannot go out there!" Said Du-Whop.

"He has my brother; I have to go!"

"It's a trap son!"

"You think I don't know that!" Damien snapped. "I don't care if it's a trap, I'm not going to leave him out there to die while I sneak out of the back door!"

"Damien if you just wait a minute! I have a plan." Du-Whop spoke with a sincerity Damien had never heard. The priest's

words suddenly sprang back to mind. A guardian angel huh?
Well, what else did Damien have to lose?

"Alright, what do we do."

PART III

The doors of the church creaked open slowly. The cool night air rushed in along with the smell of blood and pain. There was a clear path to the street from the entrance of the church, not a single sign of the wolves anywhere, and for a moment Damien hoped that maybe that he had imagined it all, like some type of horrible living nightmare.

Art stepped out of the doorway first, the shotgun gripped tightly in his hands. Damien was close behind him, armed with the snub nose. Du-Whop was supposed to bring up the rear. At least that was the plan. The idea was for both Du-Whop and Art to sandwich Damien in between them. Art and would carry his shotgun and Damien the snub nose, if any of the werewolves got to close Art would fire first, hoping to score a hit at point blank range, which they were, in turn, were hoping would translate into a dead werewolf. Whenever Art had to stop and reload Damien would fend the wolves off with the snub nose, aiming for the head. They knew the smaller gun couldn't kill a wolf, not even up close, but they really only needed to buy a little time, get the wolves to hesitate for a moment so that Art could reload. And if everything went right, kill another wolf.

For the most part that was the plan, at least as far as Damien understood it. Apparently, as they killed two of the werewolves Du-Whop had one last ace in the hole to deal with the last wolf, he didn't seem to think it was necessary to tell Damien the details though. Simply once they got down to one wolf, Art and Damien could grab Rell and run for the cars still parked in the back of the church. Damien didn't argue, one suicide plan worked just as good as the next as far as he was concerned, as long as the words "Grab Rell" were included, he figured he could make the rest work. As a result, he admittedly didn't focus to closely on the details, they didn't matter. That is until he stepped outside of the church into the cold night air and practically into the jaws of man-eating wolf monsters, and suddenly, suddenly the details became very important.

Damien followed closely behind Art, with the expectation that Du-Whop was following closely behind him. He wasn't. Damien's back was bare, and he looked back to see the old addict closing the church doors leaving both him and Art literally to the wolves.

"Du-Whop you fucking junkie bastard?! WHAT ARE YOU DOING?" Damien had half a mind to bolt back to the church doors. But a sharp elbow from Art stopped him.

"Ay there boyo, stick to the plan!"

"Plan?! There is no plan Du-Whop sent us out here as dog food!" Damien continued to look back over his shoulder as the church doors slammed shut. Before they closed, he could see small motes of light dancing behind the head of Du-Whop, lights independent of the lights that illuminated the church. Damien found himself even more confused than he thought possible, right up until.

"HAHAHAHAHA!" A grizzled and merciless laugh cut into his train of thought. "It is so pathetic how the sheep scramble in the face of death." Hector's voice seemed to speak from everywhere and nowhere all at the same time. Damien looked in every direction but still could not find the source. "Damien, the more you struggle, the more painful this will be."

Without warning one of the werewolves appeared to the left of both Damien and Art. Damien spotted it first, he aimed the small revolver at it, pointing at its head. His finger curled around the trigger and right before he could fire Art's shotgun exploded with a resounding boom. Damien watched as the left side of the wolf's face was sheared from its skull. The gigantic animal fell to the ground writhing in agony, it didn't appear to be dead, but it was down, it was wounded, and now they could move in and finish it off quickly.

"One down." Damien thought and for a moment. He had a small glimmer of hope, a solitary thought that they may actually be able to survive the ordeal, and almost as quickly as the thought arrives, it runs away in sheer terror as Damien can feel the hot breath of what he can only assume to be another of the werewolves breathing on the back of his neck. Damien turned to find himself staring directly into the maw of the large humanoid wolf, its mouth pulled back into a blood-curdling snarl, white foam and sharp teeth displayed between thin black lips. The werewolf pushed out a harsh snort through its shimmering canine nose, and hot wet breath sprayed onto Damien's face. Any thoughts he had of surviving died in that moment and slowly he felt himself rising out of his own body as if his soul had already begun the departure process in anticipation of the gruesome and painful end that was undoubtedly about to ensue. Before he could drift too far away, he felt a hard tug on the collar of his shirt and Art's voice screamed to him "Get Down." and in his peripheral vision, he saw the barrel of the shotgun move toward the growling werewolf. He rushed to cover his ears and head before the gun barrel boomed in the direction of the monster. The gunshot jolted him back to life. He looked back in the direction of the wolf hoping to find another carcass missing half ahead but instead found nothing. The wolf had not only dodged the shot it had vanished altogether.

"Damien, I have lost two men, you have only lost one... You see, that's what I like about you, you are a survivor." Hector's voice spoke directly from behind them now, Damien and Art turned with both guns aimed out in front of them. Damien expected to find more empty space again and was rather surprised to see the wolf version of Hector standing there with

Rell gripped between his claws. "Well more like one and a half."
The wolf said, "But what do you say? Shall we even the odds?"

Art cocked the shotgun and took aim, and in one fluid
motion, Hector heaved Rell's body directly into the priest. And
no sooner than the wounded Rell left his grip, Hector had once
again vanished from sight. Rell crashed into Art who was
knocked down on to his back by the force and weight of the half-
unconscious Rell. Damien attempted to dash out of the way of
the collision taking place in front of him and stumbled backward
and began flailing toward the face of the church trying
desperately not to fall. As if on cue the other werewolf skid into
view. It bounded on all fours toward Damien with inhuman
speed closing the distance between the two of them faster than
Damien could think. He raised his gun and squeezed the trigger
hard, it fired but missed its mark. Damien watched the bullet
strike the ground a few feet passed the wolf which had become
airborne as it leaped forward to pounce on its prey. Damien knew
that he could fire the gun a hundred more times and hit the
werewolf dead center mass and it would be enough to stop its
momentum at this point. For what he tallied to be at least the
fifth time that night, he was sure he was about to die.

Damien lifted the gun in futility and fired every round
available, the monster seemed to absorb the bullets more so than
be struck by them, and its huge body moved in what felt like slow
motion as it fell upon Damien. Before the werewolf could crush
him under its massive weight, it was snatched out of the air by
something of a similar form. A larger wolf with spotty grey and
black fur tackled the bounding wolf in mid-air. The two animals
rolled through the air and hit the ground with a welp. The
scrambled to their feet, the wolf that Damien shot moving only
slightly faster than the newcomer, not that it did much good. The
shot werewolf reared back to attack the patchy black and grey
one, only to be smacked downward with a ferocious paw that
sent the thing face first into the pavement, and with a savagery

that could only belong to a creature of human intelligence the patchy grey and black werewolf begin to mercilessly pound and smash the head of the younger looking monster, until its limp body lay motionless and lifeless in the shadow of the church entrance.

Damien froze, the large wolfman raised to its hind legs. Its movements much more human than the other wolves they had encountered that night. Its fur was matted and mangy, its dull black coat was blotched with large swaths of grey, signs of age. An observation Damien would have noted had he been functioning within his right mind. However, he was not. He was now in a mental state of confusion that surpassed all levels of confusion previously ever known. He was being hunted by werewolves, yet somehow, he had just been saved by a werewolf. Hunted by werewolves, saved by a werewolf. Damien's mind imploded within itself. He looked at the large spotty wolf, then looked back to Art. The priest was wrestling himself from underneath Rell and seemed utterly unfazed by the arrival of a new and apparently "friendly" werewolf. He laid down the hostage that had just been thrown at him like a rag doll. Jumped up with the shotgun in hand and took aim at the wolf he had wounded earlier. Damien looked down at his target expecting to see a half dead werewolf, but instead saw a half-dead werewolf that was very quickly regrowing its missing face and very rapidly becoming once again a very live werewolf. The wolf was regenerating, and at the same time it was slowly crawling toward Rell and Art, still stalking its prey with half of its skull exposed. Art stood over the wounded werewolf and right as it's regenerating muscle wrapped itself around its exposed skull, Art pulled the shotgun trigger and werewolf's head exploded.

Art looked up to see both Damien and the splotchy werewolf watching him, he smiled. "Lou! Good to see you're back to your old self!"

Damien looked back to the wolf. "Du-Whop? You- you're a werewolf?!"

Du-Whop looked at Damien from his wolf form, then looked down at his own hands, fur covered hands with long nail-like claws at the end of each finger moved at his command. He flexed his arms, staring down at himself as if he were getting reacquainted with the movement and feel of his own body.

"Yes," he said, "I am." Du-Whop's voice, much like Hector's, was human in note but carried with it a primal and savage undertone that made Damien shudder from the mere sound of it.

"Explanations later! Keep your guard up, there is one more bloody wolf lef..."

Art stopped talking mid-speech and looked down. There was a large red claw protruding from his stomach, actually upon closer inspection, there were two claws, set in opposing directions. And with a growl, the two claws ripped themselves apart severing Art into two complete halves in the process. Art's body fell to the ground in two loud wet slumps, now much more meat than man.

"Art?" Damien stammered; the words barely able to escape his lips.

"Nooooooo!" Du-Whop growled and screamed at the same time.

"Tonight has simply been full of surprises" Hector spoke with a demonic chuckle in his wolf throat. The werewolf pointed one of his blood-soaked claws at the transformed Du-Whop. "I don't know who you are or how you managed to hide your true... nature, from me. But I will have you know this; I am here under strict instructions from the Pack Lord himself. Whatever your aims, whatever orders you may be acting under, they have been overridden. The boy is to come with me, the Master commands it, and what the Master commands a wolf must obey."

"Unlike you," Du-Whop growled in a harsh whisper, "I SERVE NO MASTER!" Du-Whop burst forward lunging out at Hector with claws and teeth. The two werewolves crashed into one another with the force of two titans. With sheer brute strength, Du-Whop forced Hector off of his feet and slammed the monster onto his back. Hector reacted instantly and used the momentum of their fall to launch Du-Whop over his head with a monkey flip. Du-Whop flew through the air, bounced off the ground, and twisted mid bounce and right himself back up to all fours in what seemed like a flash. Hector was also back up, and the two werewolves circled one another, each of them looking for the smallest opportunity to gain the advantage on the other.

"Why are you still here?" Du-Whop growled; his eyes still glued to Hector. "Now is your chance, grab Rell and go. Run Damien, Now!" On his last word, Du-Whop lunged at Hector once again, who had only momentarily looked away in an attempt to keep an eye on Damien before he began to flee, it was all the opening that Du-Whop needed. He was on top of Hector before he could react, biting and clawing at him ferociously. Hector bit back, and more than once swiped his large claws across Du-Whop's canine face, large open wounds were left in their wake, wounds that begin to heal themselves almost immediately as they were created.

Damien awoke from the daze he was in and leaped into action. He still didn't know what the hell was going on, but this would be the best chance he had of getting Rell and himself out of this situation alive. He rushed to Rell side, who still lay where Art had left him. Damien found him slowly stirring, struggling to come back to consciousness but still very unaware of their present situation.

"Rell, Rell wake up."

"Wha... What the fu-"

"Get up we have to go!" Damien helped Rell sit up, then threw an arm around his shoulder.

"Aye shit D, I can't, I can't move, my leg, it's broke."

"Nigga, get yo ass up, we gotta get out of here!" Damien hefted Rell to his feet to which Rell responded with a pained gasp. "Come on we just have to make it to the truck." The two of them begin to hobble forward. They moved slowly at first then quickly begin to pick up the pace. "Yo we gon be fine yo, we can make it," Damien whispered words of encouragement between breaths. "It's all good, we got this, this is just like that three-legged race we won in Mrs. Tennabern class in fourth grade, remember?"

"D shut up and let's just get the hell out of here!" Rell forced out with a laugh. "Forget Mrs. Tennabern!"

"Well bring you crippled ass on then!"

Rell let out exasperated laughs between wincing grunts of pain.

The boys' brotherly reunion was short lived once Damien looked back over his shoulder. Hector and Du-Whop were still fighting; however, Hector now seemed to be gaining the upper hand. A heavy punch to the back of the head sent Du-Whop to the ground, he moved slowly, struggling to get back to his feet. Hector delivered another kick to the head. At the sight of which, Damien urged Rell to hobble faster. Hector looked to the two retreating boys and began bounding toward them.

"Rell run faster!"

"Huh?"

"The werewolf is on its way fool, run faster!"

Rell looked back over his shoulder, cursed under his breath and tried as best he could to hobble faster.

Hector began to dash forward once again on all fours closing the gap between him and Damien quickly and efficiently. Damien and Rell had made it to the side of the church, but they were still some 50 feet away from the nearest vehicle and at the rate they were moving, they had little to no chance of making it before being mauled and very likely eaten by the pursuing werewolf. Hector had closed maybe half the distance between himself and his prey when he once again felt the digging claws and teeth sink into his back. The old werewolf was on him once again.

"This damned old man is persistent." he thought. "But how? How was he still fighting, or better yet, how was he acting independently of the pack? All lycanthropes were beholden to one master, and his will was law, to disobey, to defy him meant a pain so unimaginable that death was the only reprieve. But this old man, this old man was free. Free and acting of his own volition and he was using that freedom to protect this boy. Risking his life for this boy. The master's request must not have been without merit. There must be something very special about Damien Sills." Hector decided then, he would kill the old rogue werewolf, and take this potential back to his master gift wrapped and with a bow, after all, it was his master's will, and when the master commands, a wolf must obey.

The werewolves re-collide, biting in clawing. Intertwined in one another and moving like a tornado of fur and teeth. In the midst of the melee, Hector found an opening and with great delight sunk his large teeth into the side of Du-Whops neck. Blood sprayed in all directions. In a burst of pain-laden strength,

Du-Whop pulled away allowing Hector's teeth to drag across his flesh ripping and tearing the wound even further, mounds of blood begin to spill forth from the gaping hole in Du-Whops neck.

Killing a werewolf was difficult, and even though Du-Whop was old, it had not necessarily meant he was weaker, in fact, it was quite the opposite. Though he was not as fast, or as agile as Hector, Du-Whops seniority as a lycanthrope gave him significant benefits that could not be shortchanged. His hide was tough, and while Hector could scratch it, his claws were not strong enough to punch through and do any significant damage to any internal organs, Du-Whop's bones were dense and heavy, breaking them was nearly impossible and the crushing of his skull in the same way the old wolf had done to one of Hector's soldiers was out of the question. No, when brute strength was not on your side, the only way one werewolf could kill another was purely through a test of endurance. All werewolves, even the elder ones had a finite limit to its regenerative capabilities. The longer a battle stretched and the more damage and abuse the wolf's body underwent the slower it would begin to heal until eventually, the wolf's body would stop healing itself altogether. Once a wolf lost its ability to heal itself, they often bleed out from their remaining injuries. Hector could see that the old wolf-man was reaching his limits. Hell, even his body was beginning to feel the effects of battle fatigue. The bites and scratches on his body lingered much longer then he was comfortable with, blood trickled down from open wounds that simply refused to close, his muscle burned and ached in ways that he had not felt in years. If he was beginning to feel the signs of exhaustion the old man had to be preparing to drop at any moment.

Du-Whops clawed hand gripped tightly around the wound on his neck, he squeezed and pressed as hard as he could, but it seemed to do nothing to staunch the blood flow. He swayed back and forth, then took a step backward. Hector couldn't tell if he was trying to move away from him intentionally or simply try to catch himself from falling. He assumed it was the latter, the old dog had come too far to turn tail and run now. He was either too proud or too stupid to run away from a fight. Probably both, Hector thought. He spat out a mouth full of blood in disapproval. The old fool's attachment and loyalty to this boy had gotten him killed. Such a waste, a liberated lycanthrope of his rank could have gone off and started pack of his own. Or perhaps, maybe that's what he was trying to do.

Maybe the boy was being groomed for that purpose, perhaps he was fighting so hard because he was trying to protect the future of his own lycanthropic bloodline. That would explain his fervor, his absolutely unwavering determination in the face of what assuredly had to be his imminent death. Even now, barely able to stand, the old wolf bared his teeth and growled with such ferocity. He looked like he couldn't even see straight, but still Hector dare not get to close without a clear and decisive opening, after all, it could be a feint, the old dog could be faking it hoping to lull Hector into a false sense of security, get him to let his guard down, and perform a counterattack that had Hector holding his own throat trying to will his regeneration back into full effect before it was too late. No, Hector had been around too long, had grown too strong and come too far to lose it all in a solitary act of arrogance. Besides, the night, with all its trouble and hiccups, had brought something extremely valuable Hector's way. The old man had introduced a thought that had never even occurred to Hector before, a thing that he had never even thought possible. This old dog had brought to Hector, the possibility of freedom. The idea that he could somehow free himself from the master and possibly even start his own pack, well that was easily worth the four werewolves he had lost on this damned mission. Hell, that information was worth one hundred werewolves as far as Hector was concerned. And now that he knew it was possible, he was determined not to rest until he found out how. But between now and then he had to play the role of a good soldier and stay well within the master's favor. And that started with retrieving this boy.

Du-Whop dropped to one knee, he couldn't even stand, but he was still in his wolf form which meant he was still dangerous. Hector had to make a quick decision. Move in for the kill and do away with the rogue here and now or leave him to bleed out and go for the boy before he got any further away. Hector stared at the old wolf, He was soaked in blood, and his body heaved up and down as he struggled to pull in air. He was dying for sure. But Hector also noticed that even in his squatted position, his muscles were still clenched tight, and he knew better than anyone that a wolf backed into a corner could still lash out with desperate and deadly force. It was a mistake that he had already made once tonight, but in his mind, it was the best-calculated risk he could think of. He turned his back on the weathered and blood soak lycanthrope to give chase to the boy. Let the old dog bleed out, his threat was minimal at a distance, and he would be in no condition to be giving chase anytime soon. "It's best to let dying dogs die." Hector thought, and with that, he turned away from Du-Whop, and his eyes fell upon Damien and Rell some 40 feet away, scrambling to make their way to the vehicle he himself had arrived in.

"Go go go go go go go go!" Damien hobbled and muttered at the same time. He looked back over his shoulder one more time and noted it looked like they were a decent distance away. "Looks like... looks like Du-Whop bought us some time. This is our chance, we gotta go now."

"Good, good we're almost there."

And they were, the boys were only some ten feet from Hector's SUV. Damien felt the familiar swell of hope bubble up inside himself, they could do it, they could survive this awful night and somehow put it all behind them. Then without warning, Rell pushed hard against Damien's left side, slipped his grip and heaved his body on top of what used to be Jake and the werewolf that he managed to kill before dying, only now the werewolf had turned back to a human.

"Rell, what the hell are you doing?"

Rell dug around between the bodies for a brief moment, then outstretched one arm gripping something between his thumb and forefinger.

"Car keys," Rell said. "This was the one how hopped out of the driver's seat."

"Well aren't you a genius" Damien reached down and pulled his friend back up to one foot. He noticed that Rell was also holding Jake's gun as well.

"Come on let's get the hell out of here," Rell said.

They moved quickly over to the empty SUV. Damien yanked open the back door and with a forceful push heaved his friend into the back seat. Rell slid in, back first, propped his broken leg on to the seat and painfully pulled himself back across the seat. Damien tried to help as best he could without putting to much pressure on the broken leg, and then suddenly, Damien stopped with a jolt, and before Rell could ask "What's wrong?" Damien was yanked forcefully away from the car.

Hector grabbed hold to Damien's ankle and snatched him from the door of the vehicle. He had almost gotten away. Probably would have, if he hadn't been trying to drag his wounded friend along with him. Hector held the boy up by his leg dangling him aloft and upside down. He leaned in closer for a better look at this child that had caused him so much trouble in a single night. There was nothing to see necessarily, but Hector could feel and even smell the potential, he had raw, unrefined energy surging within him. For a haggard and exhausted werewolf, he would make a filling meal. The energy dwelling within him would send Hector's regeneration abilities right back to their peak, but for those same reasons, Hector knew the boy would make an even better convert. Hector released the boy's leg, but before he could hit the ground the werewolves same hand darted out like a lightning bolt and grabbed hold to the collar of Damien's shirt. In a single motion, flipping him right-side-up and now holding him by the nape of his neck like a dog holds a puppy. Hector brought the boy close to his own face before speaking.

"Oh Damien, you were so close to getting away, had you left that friend of yours behind you perhaps could have made it a bit further. I'll never understand why you people form such attachments to a worthless and useless thing like friendship. Ah well, now you will be coming with me, and just to assure you that escape won't be an option this time..." Hector used his free hand to grab hold of Damien's right wrist, extended his arm, and then chomped down hard on the boy's right shoulder. The werewolf's massive jaws covered everything from Damien's shoulder to his collarbone. Hector tightened his jaw just enough to feel his teeth puncture the skin and streams of blood begin to spray from beneath the teeth. Damien screamed out in pain. The boy's warm blood hit the werewolf's mouth, and tongue and even from the mere taste of it Hector could feel a small surge of power flow through him. A werewolf derives his power from consuming the flesh of humans, and the flesh of some humans, those with potential, contained much more power and energy than others. From the small taste of blood alone Hector could tell this boy had something special, this is what the master wanted, this is what the old man was protecting. To feed on one such as this would be a waste, Damien would make an exceedingly powerful werewolf. Hector bit down a little harder, unto he felt and heard the audible pop of a shoulder being dislodged from its socket.

Damien yelled out again, and at the same time, Hector's jaws released him.

"...That should slow you down a bit," he growled to the boy, releasing his shirt and letting him fall to the grown. He hit the hard pavement already clutching his arm, writhing in agony.

"And now, to deal with this 'friend' of yours." Hector turned back toward the SUV, he wondered for a moment, perhaps he should blood test the friend as well. Potentials did tend to attract one another, and Damien seemed about as dumb for this friend of his as the old man was for him. It was worth a shot, after all, if he proved to be nothing special, Hector could always simply eat him. Hector stepped into the doorway of the open vehicle to see surprisingly enough Rell sitting upright and with a very large gun pointed directly at Hector's face. It looked alarmingly like the gun that had killed two of his men earlier that night and at this range, it would be dangerously close to doing the same to him.

"He ain't going nowhere with you, you dog-faced son of a bi-"

The werewolf craned his head hard to the left while at the same time swatting at the gun with his large oversized claws. He knocked the gun from Rell's hand but not before the boy was able to fire a single shot. The gun exploded loudly and violently before it was swept away. Flames leaped from the barrel propelling along with it, a bullet that narrowly missed going between Hector's eyes. Instead, it ripped up along the right side of his face, grazing over his snout, passing by his eye and then fully taking his right ear clean off the side of his head. The wolf howled in an agony of his own now, he stumbled back away from the open car door, holding his fur covered face, blood pouring from the laceration the stray bullet had cut across it.

"Why you little bastard, I'll rip your throat ou-" Hector stopped, he tried looking out of his good eye but could not makes sense of what he was seeing. It was Du-Whop, he was standing over Damien, and it looked like he was licking the boys wounded shoulder, or, no... wait, was he lapping up his blood, but how, he should have bled out, he was all but dead, there's no way.

As if hearing his thought, the old wolf's head turned, all of his thick dagger-like teeth showing. He looked beyond enraged, beyond inhuman, almost feral. An animal of his size and his strength without the tempered sentience of a human was, in every way beyond terrifying.

A desperate wolf always has one last attack, and somehow, Hector had allowed Du-Whop to become more desperate than himself. The old dog was already coiled to strike, and before Hector could think to react, Du-Whop pounced, lunging out at him and clapping his jaws down on the werewolf neck. His jaws shut, clenched and locked down like a vice, crunching mangling and shredding everything between them. Hector felt his windpipe close shut, then felt it punctured by razor sharp teeth, blood poured out filling his lungs and mouth. He felt his throat collapse, and it felt like he had swallowed his own tongue, but he knew he hadn't, because he could still feel it dangling from a mouth that he could no longer control. He felt Du-Whops jaws slam shut exactly where his throat used to be, and then he could feel the old one's front teeth clamp together and audible crunch of his own spinal cord snapping, and then... and then he felt nothing at all, and everything went black.

Du-Whop held the limp body of Hector in his jaws, then opened them and the red-stained werewolf dropped in a heap at his feet. The old wolf sloughed forward, and then he fell face first a few feet away from where Damien stood.

"Whop! Whop you did it you killed him. Whop get up, come on you can go now." Damien kneeled down next to the old man in the shape of a large lupine beast. Du-Whop rolled over to his back, he was covered in bites and scratches, his fur soaked and matted with blood, a large wound on his neck pulsed in what seemed to be in rhythm with his heartbeat, blood gushed forward with each pump. Damien put a hand over it, to try and slow the flow. He could only use his left hand, Du-Whop had set his right shoulder back into place, and then had even licked the wounds which had somehow managed to dull the pain, but it was still all but useless. "Yo Whop, heal this shit and let's get out of here. You did it, you beat him, you saved us."

Rell hopped forward from the open car, he was on one foot. "D, what are you doing? We have to leave."

"Aye, no, Rell this is Du-Whop, we need to, we have to carry him, we have to get him in the truck."

"That's what?"

"It's Du-Whop, he's a werewolf, it's hard to explain. Just, help me... help me get him up."

Without question, Rell took another hop forward and began trying to bend down.

Du-Whop reached out and grabbed hold to Damien's wrist.

"Nah young blood," he spoke in a low grumbled tone, his voice still drowning with the wolf's signature growl but still distinctly Du-Whop. "I think I'll just lay here for a while. You boys... you boys gon and go."

"Man we ain't leaving you here!"

"You ain't got no choice, besides you ain't leaving me, I'm holding up the rear, watching your back as you get away. You know it ain't no thang for me baby boy, I'm a survivor." Du-Whop coughed, and blood sprayed from his mouth.

"Whop you are fucking dying bro, we gotta get you out of here." Damien sounded as if he was pleading.

"Whop let us help you, man you know we can't leave you like this." Rell chimed in.

"Y'all wanna know how y'all can help me... Leave. Go, right now. You can help me by surviving. Leave New Hampton, leave the life behind, go! This is... this is far from over, the ones that came after you tonight, there will be more. They'll keep coming, and they won't stop until they catch you, or kill you. So, if you want to do something for me, I just ask that you boys survive. Survive for me that will be enough. My time here is done, but as long as you two keep moving forward, I'm fine with that."

Damien stood up and took a single step back. He saw on Du-Whop's face what he only could assume to be a smile.

"D, Rell, go to Bridgeport. Find a man named Charles Blackhill, he helped me a long time ago, and he can help y'all too, both of you. Promise me, promise me you'll find him."

"We will Whop, we'll find him."

"Good, really good. Now go, get out of here and remember, remember everything I said."

Slowly and reluctantly the two boys hobbled over to the open SUV, loaded themselves inside and with a mournful look in their eyes, drove away.

Du-Whop still lay on his back, he had a clear, unobstructed view of the night sky. The moon was full that night. He loved the moon. He heard a dog howl in the distance. He took a deep breath and noticed that he had actually turned back to his human form. He looked back up to the moon, smiled to himself and closed his eyes.

Part IV

Hurried footsteps made their way to the side of Du-Whop's outstretched body, and before long a fresh-faced and unruffled Art kneeled down by the side of his old friend.

"Bloody hell..." Art put a hand on Du-Whops arm, he was cold. "Rest easy now old friend, your work here is complete."

Across from Art, iridescent motes of light begin to bob and dance over his shoulder. The lights moved faster and faster with each passing second until they danced so rapidly that they almost appeared to form the solid shape. The shape of a man wrapped in glowing strands of light. Then suddenly, with a piercing flash, the dancing lights faded away and, in their place, stood another Art.

The original Arthur didn't bother to look up and without prompting the new Arthur spoke.

"We can't risk falling too far behind. You go, I'll take care of him."

The original Art stood up and removed the priest collar from around his neck.

"We've got things from here Lou I'll watch over your boys for you."

-

Evolutionary

Episode 1: Welcome to the New World

I woke up with the distinctively irritating feeling of sand in my mouth. Sand and blood, the two formed a horrible combination when mixed, and also an overwhelming feeling of nausea when you had no idea where either of them had come from. I managed to pull myself up to my feet. At a complete loss for where I was, or how I had gotten there, I did the only thing I could think to do and begin to walk toward the setting sun.

From the inside, all deserts look the same. My mind scrambled trying to remember or recall, which one I was currently in. The Sahara, the Mojave, the Gobi; was I dropped out of a plane, did I escape from some remote facility or did I just randomly pop out of the sand? I had no history, no memories, no nothing. Amnesia in the truest sense, and it sucked. Then again, I couldn't even faithfully call it amnesia, as far as I knew 20 minutes ago, I didn't exist. To have amnesia you have to have a past at least, you just don't remember what it is, but when you've just popped up out of the sand, you don't have a past. You're just there.

I checked my person for equipment or clues as to my identity. Heavy duty work pants, made from a chemically treated fabric, a cotton polyester blend, tough enough to offer me ample protection from the elements without stifling or restricting my movement. They were apparently designed for such conditions. How I knew this, was a mystery to me. Perhaps I was a tailor in a past life, either way, the pockets were empty, and I was still, in a word, clueless. I was wearing a matching jacket made from the same technologically advanced material as the pants, and though the heat beamed, I zipped up the jacket. Protection from the sun and sand was more important than a little sweat.

My feet sank deep into the shifting desert floor with every step. I stumbled over dune after dune with no particular destination in mind.

After walking for what seemed like hours, I could see, what I assumed to be, a group of crudely constructed buildings in the far distance. My excitement grew as the buildings turned out to be actual solid objects and not merely symptoms of my oncoming madness from the extended exposure to the sweltering heat and a complete lack of water. I picked up my speed, and by the time the sinking sun began to near the horizon; I was closing in on what looked to be some type of abandoned village, a ghost town. The collision of the Sun and Earth turned the world a brilliant color orange, setting the tone for the ominous showdown that was about to ensue.

By the time I hit the empty village the unbearable heat had done a complete 180 degree turn and had suddenly become mind-numbingly cold, the only feeling of consistency was my unwavering thirst and the translucent orange tint that covered everything visible to the naked eye as the sun sank deeper behind the strange planet's distant curving peak. I entered the ghost town in a frenzy. I stumbled clumsily through the dirt and grit of the small plot of civilization that someone, at some point in time, had probably considered a settlement. The scene was desolate, to say the least. The air smelled heavily of abandonment, the buildings and city structures showed multiple signs of neglect. It seemed not to have been populated by a living soul in years, perhaps decades, there was no real way for me to know, but in my current state, it was safe to say I didn't care. Banging on the first door I came across; I began frantically calling out for help and begging some unseen Samaritan for water. Though in my heart, I knew I truly expected no one to answer my call. More than anything I believe I was screaming only to say, once I died, that I did indeed fight desperately for my own survival. Sad, I know.

I reached for the door handle of a small shabby hovel of wood and stone, only to find it tightly locked. This surprised me, and against my better judgment, a small glimmer of hope sparked from deep within my stomach. If someone thought to lock the door than that meant, that same someone might still be inside. I pressed my face against the smooth wood, it was warm! I heard the sound of shuffling feet on the other side, someone was there!

"Hey!" My voice cracked and trembled as my throat screamed for some type of moisture. "Is anybody there?! I-I was out in the desert; I just need some water, maybe something to eat! I-I-I can pay! Please, I have money!" I lied. My pockets were empty, my primary goal was to get that door open, the details, I figured, could be worked out after I avoided dying of thirst, hunger or hypothermia.

I begin to bang even harder. My life depended on it. "Hey! Open this door, are you going to let me die out here! I'm asking you for help."

"Please," a soft whimper came from the other side of the closed door. "Please go away, we can't help you."

"Is someone there?" the sound of another voice calmed my frantic pounding and yelling, it wasn't until hearing the comfort of another sentient life form that I realized how lonely and afraid I had been, and now, how absolutely crazy I must have sounded.

"Please, please, please I understand. I just need some water. I woke up alone in the desert, I've been walking for hours, just some water please that's all I ask. Just some water and then… and then I'll leave."

The voice on the other side went quiet, the shuffling stopped. Perhaps a few seconds passed without a single sound from the inside of the door. I begin to wonder if I had imagined the shuffling, imagined the voice and I begin to panic, the feeling of dread and a fear of loneliness begin to set back in. The only thing worse than dying of thirst and starvation in the middle of nowhere is going insane before dying of thirst and starvation in the middle of nowhere. I began beating on the door again, determined to make the phantom voice appear once more. "Hey! Hey!" I screamed as loud as my voice would allow. "Are you still in there?"

"Please," the phantom voice returned even softer than before "You have to be quiet, if I give you water do you promise to leave"

"Yes," I responded without hesitation. At that point, I would have agreed to anything, anything for the promise of water and to keep the voice from disappearing again. "I'll leave, I promise just please, please give me some water."

"Sister, no!" another voice from behind the door emerged.

"Be quiet, if he keeps banging and screaming, he'll attract them for sure, this is the only way."

It wasn't until I heard the other voice, which sounded distinctly like that of a young boy that I was able to appreciate the gentleness and femininity of the phantom voice fully. It was a soothing and mellow sound, and for a moment I allowed its rhythmic melody to dance in my mind, focusing more on its beauty, as opposed to the actual words. As it turns out, I should have been a lot more focused on the "them" and finding out exactly why they were so hell-bent on not "attracting" their attention. Regretfully now I admit, I did not.

Once again, the shuffling stopped. The locks on the door began to unlatch themselves, and slowly the door crept open, I breathed a sigh of relief, followed quickly and swiftly by a gasp of complete and utter horror.

The door opened slightly to reveal standing behind it, an ape, peeking out from around the edge of the door. And then, right before I could even let out a girlish scream of absolute terror that I had lodged in my throat, it spoke.

"Well, what are you waiting for, come in!" She whispered. She? It was her; the phantom voice was the ape girl. The room began to spin, maybe it was the sudden drop in temperature, the lack of water, or whatever extenuating circumstance that brought me to this strange and terrible place, but my fragile mind had reached its breaking point, and right before it passed into oblivion, I managed to choke out the words

"You're a monkey." And with that, I begin a face-first descent into the cold hard wooden floor of the doorway. I passed out before I hit the ground.

Episode 2: The Mild Mannered and the Mentally Ill

My eyes fluttered open, but my vision was a mish-mash of blurry, indecipherable images that my frazzled mind was in no mood to try and make sense of. As a result, my first impression of my surroundings came from auditory and tactile senses instead. The first set of stimuli was tactile. I lay supine, splayed out across the floor. A hard-wooden floor; cold and bare, it seemed like the type of floor that did not particularly liked being stepped upon, and without question loathed being laid upon, and as a result, its hardness and coldness was unforgiving in its interaction with my poor back. My head, however, my head was being cradled and sat nestled gently and quite comfortably against something both soft and firm. Something which radiated from it, a soothing warmth that can only be generated from the body of another living thing. A tender hand ran itself from the front to the back of my head. The gentle motion had a ripple effect that sent waves of calming energy through my body so even though I was terribly confused, I found myself still extremely relaxed and under the impression that I was, if not already dead, at the very least, quite safe. The second set of stimuli was auditory. Voices, similar to the ones that I had heard from the other side of the door.

"I told you not to open the door, now he's in here having fits all over our floor!" said a small boy like voice.

"Who is the older sibling, you or I?"

"At times Sister, I honestly cannot tell."

"Quiet, I think he's waking."

"Why do I ha-,"

"Shhh,"

Slowly my eyes regained focus and the sights before me gradually coalesced into solid objects. I was laying on the floor, in the lap of a woman... in the lap of the same woman that had opened the door, the woman with the face of a...

"Monkey!" I shouted the word out loud. My eyes as wide as plates and my voice cracked and hoarse from lack of hydration. I must have startled her because when I yelled, she jumped and, in the process, dropped my head to the hard floor. It hit the ground with a thud, and I groaned in pain, grabbing the back of my head as it bounced off the unforgiving wood.

"Serves you right, you know that term is rude and offensive, especially considering I just saved your life. I do have a name you know."

I scrambled to my feet and then scuttled backward like a beach crab until I found myself in a corner of the room and could go no further.

"But-but, you are. You're a mon-"

"I am an Ape, thank you very much. A She-Ape as if you couldn't tell, and quite frankly I don't think I have ever met anyone so crass and so crude as to go out of his way to insult the lady that attempted to help him in his time of need."

I stopped my panicking and paused for a second. She was an ape, and from all indications, she was a she, or at least she dressed like a she. She was wearing a dress, a green dress, that draped across her shoulders and torso like a vest and across the chest a pair of strings zig-zagged from the waist up and were tied into a neat bow just beneath her collarbone, under the dress she wore a white linen blouse whose long sleeves stretched out to her wrist. The back of her hands were covered in a thick dark fur, from which, long thin, hairless fingers protruded out. The dress ran down to her ankles, and from the bottom of it, small black shoes with silver buckles peered from underneath. Her head was covered in the same thick black fur as her hands, with the exception of her face, an undeniably simian face. A flat nose, an almost no existent nose, actually it was more like two nostrils sat in the middle of her face. And above them lay bright green eyes and below them a cupped mouth and thin lips that seemed to cover large over-sized teeth. The woman, or Ape-woman, in front of me, looked, for all intents and purposes, insulted, and in some odd way, genuinely hurt.

"I-I'm sorry," I choked out.

"Well that's for sure." she snapped in retort.

"I told you we should never have opened the door."

I looked up, to see, standing on a flight of stairs, a small Ape-boy.

I am ashamed to say at the sight of him I let out a small "Eeep!" of surprise, but in an attempt to cause no further offense I quickly brought my hands up to cover my mouth.

I looked back at the Ape-Woman who was now looking at me even more bewildered than before.

"Why, you act as if you've never seen an Ape before."

"I-I haven't," I squeaked.

"Are you ill?" She asked, with what now seemed like genuine concern. "Stranger... don't you know? You are an Ape."

At that point, it was either I or the room itself, that began to suddenly and violently spin. I can't entirely be sure which, I know only that, when the spinning stopped, I was in front of a mirror and I was staring at a reflection that echoed my every movement, only it stared back at me with those now, all so familiar features, flat nose, cupped mouth, thin lips the face of a what could only be described as an Ape-Man.

The room, or perhaps it was me, begin to spin again and within seconds I felt myself falling, one more time, face first to the cold hard wooden floor.

I woke up for the third time, in the span of a day, confused and disoriented. This time to what felt like a bucket full of water to the face. I choked and gagged my way back to consciousness.

"Wake up you!" the small ape-boy was standing over me, an empty bucket in his hands.

"What happened?" I asked, still spitting water from my mouth.

"You fainted," Chimed in the She-Ape.

"Again," said the boy, "After looking at your own reflection. Not that I blame you on that account, If I had a face like yours, I'd probably faint t-"

"Thomas!" spouted the girl, looking half embarrassed.

"I-I don't understand," I muttered.

"Neither do we," Thomas mumbled, more to himself than to me.

"I- I'm not supposed to be an Ape; I'm supposed to be an..." I froze. My mind went blank as I tried to reach within, and grasp hold to the words.

"You're supposed to be a what?" asked the she-ape.

My eyes raced around the room as my mind scrambled to make sense of my current predicament. I was in the desert, then I found the town, the whole time never noticing that I was an Ape, the entire time assuming I was a... what? No words, not even an idea came to me.

"You're supposed to be a what?" She asked again.

I looked up from amidst my lost thoughts.

"I don't know," I answered, and for a moment I felt as if I might pass out for the third time that day.

There was a "Hmph," from the small boy-ape but I couldn't tell if it was a sound of frustration or satisfaction.

"You've been out in the wastelands for who knows how long, you're dehydrated and probably just a bit confused. Do you remember your name?"

"My name?" I thought for a moment, and then I began to panic. I backtracked through my mind with a fine-tooth comb, and all I could recall was that damned desert. There was nothing there except sand, just sand and heat and sun.

"I-I don't remember," I said dejectedly.

"You don't even know your own name?" blurted out the ape-boy with an unabashed squeal of delight.

"Thomas I told you to be quiet!" the ape-girl snapped, to which Thomas jumped slightly, and his expression of heartfelt joy turned to mild embarrassment and then quickly to seething contempt which seemed to be for some reason aimed at me, as I imagine he held me responsible as the source of his scolding. "It's fine," the she-ape said to me, her voice once again gentle and soothing. "The heat can play terrible tricks on the mind, you probably just need some water, some food and some rest. You can stay here until you get your bearings about you."

I have no doubt the boy wanted to protest, but he said nothing.

"Could that be your name?" The Ape-girl asked pointing to a patch on the right breast of my jacket. I looked down at a set of letters staring back up at me and wondered how I hadn't noticed them before.

"Simon? Is that your name?"

Simon? The sounds of each syllable rolled through my mind like smoke. I felt parts of my brain defog, and flashes of white coats and apes in cages appeared, and also images of more apes, hairless apes, with clothes like mine.

"Yeah... Simon... that sounds, that sounds familiar," I tried to sound confident, but I was desperate to make any sense of the things going on in my head.

"Well Simon, my name is Aimee, and this is my brother Thomas." She dropped down into a squat and met me at eye level as I was still sitting huddled in the corner like a confused and scared animal, and as a result, she spoke to me as such. "You can rest here for a short while, we have water and a bit of food, but once you get your bearings, you should leave. It's not safe here."

"Not safe?" I tried pulling myself together in an effort to sound less like a bewildered child and regain some sort of dignity. I have no doubt that I failed miserably. I could still feel my voicing shaking as I spoke. "Why would it not be safe?"

Aimee stood up and quickly made her way to and then through an open archway at the far end of the room. She then returned just as quickly with a tin cup and saucer that held a slice of bread which was smattered with what looked like butter and honey. She handed me the plate. The smell of bread, butter, and honey set off something feral inside me, and I suddenly realized how hungry I was. I took the saucer and the cup, the second of which looked to be filled with water and with a great ferocity I ate and drank. I scarfed down the bread and guzzled down the water with hardly a breath in between.

"The Saurians," she said after I'd finished gorging myself, on the bread and water.

"The what?"

"The Saurians, they come weekly to collect a tax."

"Saurians? Tax? What is that like your government?"

"No..." Aimee stared at me with an even more confused look on her face than the one that she had worn before. I suddenly begin to feel as if I had grown a second head. "Where did you say you came from?" She asked, a strong look of apprehension plastered across her face. Apparently if wandering in from the desert and not knowing my own name was not enough to cause for concern, my lack of familiarity with these Saurians was.

"I didn't," I responded. "I came in from the east, following the setting sun. I must have been walking for hours."

"From the East?" Her hand moved towards her mouth as if she were trying to stop herself from saying more.

"Sister?" Thomas spoke for the first time since being scolded. "The facility father spoke of; it was to the east..."

In the back of my mind, I could hear a plodding sound, like a great rhythmic thumping.

"Facility?"

Aimee seemed hesitant to speak. "My father is a salvager, he used to go out into the wastelands looking for old Huu-Mann tech."

"Huu-Mann tech?" Once again, my mind flashed, and the hairless apes appeared in my memory, and behind them gently whirring machines, blinking lights in dimly lit rooms and amongst it all, information, endless amounts of information, so much in fact that it made little to no sense. It was all numbers and symbols, no, equations and mathematical theories, diagrams, schematics, endless amounts of information, but all of it useless, as none of it seemed to apply directly to me, none of it gave me any insight as to who I was, or where I had come from. I shook myself free of the visions.

"The Huu-Mans are an ancient civilization that used to live here a long time ago. Supposedly they were brilliant, so our father would try and find parts of their old machines and fix them. He'd only end up with old pieces of junk most times, but not too long ago he stumbled on something else, a Huu-Man facility, full of what he assumed to be machines that still worked. He went back to the facility to see what he could salvage. That was a week ago."

"Wait, wait this is- this is all so, confusing." I rubbed my hands across my face, and upon passing my forehead, my fingers slid into thick curls of coarse hair, no not hair, fur, fur that I had not noticed while out in the desert. Fur that I had not even realized I had until it was pointed out to me by Aimee and Thomas. "Where-where is this facility, the Huu-Mann facility."

"It's a day or so trek to the east, into the desert, in the direction from which you came."

My mind raced, I was remembering, but only remembering bits of nothing, perhaps if I could see this facility they spoke of, maybe it could jog some type of true understanding, perhaps it could... The plodding and thumping in my head grew louder and more intense, it was beginning to become distracting. I tried to shake it off and realized, not only could I hear it, but I could feel it, the entire room began to reverberate with the rhythmic thump of what turned out not to be solely a sound within my mind at all, no it was instead the very real sound of... of hooves.

"The Saurians!" Thomas called out with a look of horror upon his small ape face.

"Oh no," Said Aimee, "The tax..."

Episode 3: There Goes the Neighborhood

"No no no no no no nooo…" Aimee was, to say the least, in a tizzy. She dashed across the room, which I noticed for the first time, was mostly devoid of any real furniture. A full-length mirror sat in one corner of the room, and an old grandfather clock sat in another, a flight of stairs in the third and in the last me, standing there like a bump on a log. Aimee flew out of the living area, through the archway and into the room that I'd come to realize must have been their kitchen. In a matter of seconds, she reappeared with a burlap sack filled to the brim with what looked like an assortment of food, rolls of bread and wheels of cheese peeked from over the sacks topmost edge. She ran back across the empty living room and threw open the front door sitting the sack of food a few feet from where I had been standing only moments earlier. And before the door could close behind her, she was back inside and sprinting back to the kitchen once again. This time when she went through the archway, she did not immediately return. Instead, she stayed out of sight for a number of minutes, and from the kitchen I could hear rumbling and rustling as if things were being tossed around, and suddenly as I stared in the direction on which she had gone I heard a loud bang, as if something very heavy had just slammed into the floor.

The loud noise jumpstarted both Thomas and me into action, as he had also been standing unmoved since Aimee began to scramble back and forth across the cabin. The two of us now ran toward the back room, he assumingly to aide his sister, me more so out of curiosity and confusion. I poked my head through the archway and Thomas did the same. The two of us peeked around the corner to see Aimee in what looked like a food storage pantry, at her feet was another burlap sack that she was stuffing with every food item she could find, and anything that was not food was dismissively tossed aside. It was then that I saw what had fallen and made the loud banging sound. Aimee had apparently knocked over a large crate which now lay on the floor broken and spilling out of it were bulky, oddly shaped metallic shafts covered with interlocking pieces of what looked to be high-grade hard plastics. Upon seeing the broken crate and its contents, I stepped absent-mindedly into the kitchen and bent down over the crate.

"What- what is this?" I asked as I pulled out one of the metal shafts and ran my hand gently across its surface. It was cool to the touch, and on one side a small hand sized column protruded from the shaft's main body. Near it was a small lever enclosed within a metal loop that was just big enough for me to fit a finger through.

"It's scrap," said Thomas, who had already begun helping his sister stuff the remaining sack with food. "Its old Huu-Mann tech my father found, but it doesn't do anything, it's just junk."

My mind flashed. More information flooded in and for a moment my vision went blurry.

"This is a weapon," I said, almost more to myself than to them. "This is a gun."

"Well whatever it is, it doesn't work, so… it's junk." Thomas responded, picking up the now full sack of food. His sister grabbed it from his arms.

"Listen you two, we have more pressing concerns then father's old scrap collection, I have to set this by the door, and no matter what happens both of you stay inside. The Saurians do not take kindly to male apes, and they definitely would not like the idea of any new apes wandering into the town. Stay hidden stay quiet, and they should pass by quickly."

"Wait, what?" I mumbled still partly hypnotized by the thing I was holding in my hand. Aimee didn't wait for me to gather my thoughts; she blew past me running out of the kitchen and back to the front door. "You still haven't told me what the Saurians are?"

"Come see for yourself." Thomas said, pulling on the ends of my jacket and letting out a very monkey-like "ooh-ooh ah" sound almost subconsciously as if he didn't even know he had done it. I followed Thomas back into the open living area in the direction of the front door and toward a small window that looked out into the open area in the middle of the town. From the porthole-like window, I could see Aimee stepping out onto the porch and sitting down the second bag of food. But before she could duck back into the house, the heavy footfalls of hooves had arrived, and I saw the front end of a horse trot into view and riding on the back of it was a very large and very green lizard man.

"Wha-what is that!?" I clutched tightly to the gun that I forgot that I was still holding right up until that moment. I stared out the window at a monster on horseback. The green scales that covered its body glimmered when touched by the slightest hint of light, making the thing look wet and slimy even though I knew how dry and arid it was in the open air. On the top of its head was a spiny fin that rolled from front to back with a multicolored membrane that gave it the appearance of having a rainbow-colored mohawk which seemed to shutter and move of its own accord. Large bright yellow eyes with long black vertical slits sat on either side of its face. Below them protruded a snout which was tipped by two nostrils and thin reptilian lips that were curled up into a snarl revealing two rows of interlocking dagger-like teeth that looked like they were made specifically for crushing bones and rending flesh. Before I could muster up the courage to look away, a forked tongue darted from the thing's mouth and whipped upwards making a wet and slimy sweep over the monster's big yellow eyeballs. I let out a small "eep" in much of the same tone and manner that I had done earlier that day upon first meeting Aimee and Thomas. As soon as the sound escaped my throat the lizard's head jerked in my direction and I dropped down to the floor, huddled in a small ball hoping that I had not been seen.

I let the gun sit cradled in my lap as I ran my hands slowly up my face and to the back of my head all in an attempt to wake myself from the living nightmare, I had somehow gotten trapped within. "Why, why, why? Why is this happening to me?"

"Relax weirdo," Thomas whispered, "I don't think he spotted you." Thomas was standing on a small wooden crate that he had brought from the kitchen. I looked up at him from my position on the floor. He was still peeking out of the window.

"He? That thing is a he?"

"That's Malazaar, he's kind of like the ring leader. We work hard to grow food and make a life for ourselves here, and the Saurians come by ever so often to take what little we have for themselves, making it harder and harder for us to survive. That's why my father was so obsessed with the Huu-Mann tech, he says if we can get it working it'll make life a lot easier for us. He fixed one of their machines once, turned out to be a water purifier, supplied the whole town with clean water. He started collecting more and more junk after that, he was convinced that those old machines were our ticket. Huu-Manns were supposed to be really really smart, at least right up until they all died." For the first time since he had begun to talk Thomas broke his gaze from the scene outside the window and looked down at me. "But if they're all dead, then I guess they couldn't have really been all that smart after all huh?"

Thomas had what I imagine one would call a grin on his small ape face, yet, I could tell it was not a smile of joy or even smugness. He spoke like someone who was distracted as if his voice was in the room with us, but his mind was in a far-off distant place. He spoke to hide his anxiety and smiled to mask his fear. I thought about what he'd said and then looked down at the ancient machine sitting in my lap. "If they're all dead, then they couldn't have been that smart after all." My mind flashed.

"CHESTERFIELD!" A raspy voice partly hissed, partly roared and partly growled all at once, forcing me to partly pee my pants. Almost. I almost, peed my pants, the thought crossed my mind, but I will say I held it together fairly well given the circumstances.

"Oh no," muttered Thomas. "This is not good."

"What is it?"

"They spotted Aimee."

"What?" I crawled back up to my feet and peered once again out the window. Malazaar was still on the back of his horse, and I could see behind him a number of other lizard-men in an assortment of colors, two were the shade of dark brown leather, and then two more were a bright fiery orange. Each of them, with the exception of Malazaar, had dismounted their horses and were currently going from building to building picking up the respective sack, jug or barrel, that sat by the closed door of every little structure in town, each filled with, what I assumed was a tax. Each one provided by what I expected to be an additional ape family that lay hidden in their homes. Who was perhaps, as Thomas and I were, peeking silently out of their windows praying and hoping not to be seen, perhaps like Thomas they chattered away nervously in low whispers, pretending not to be afraid.

"Chesterfield!" Malazaar pulled the reins, and his horse's head flailed in the direction where Aimee stood, it began to slowly approach the porch. "Today is Tax Day, is it not?"

Aimee had a hand on the door handle, only a moment from re-entering the house, at the sound of Malazaar's voice she turned around with a spin and with her chin in the air she answered the lizard-man in a way that made me uncomfortable and, in some ways, ashamed.

"It is," she said her once gentle and low voice reinforced with new strength and steadiness that I had not heard before now.

"And how do I feel about looking at monkeys on Tax Day?"

At the sound of the word "monkey," I cringed. I knew all too well Aimee didn't like being referred to as a monkey, but I feared the consequences that would result from here attempting to openly scold the thing that stood before her. But instead of scolding, I noticed that she actually seemed a little deflated at Malazaar's last question. She took a deep breath.

"You don't like looking at monkeys on Tax Day." She said through clenched teeth.

"I don't like looking at monkeys on Tax Day, Yet! Lo and behold, I am looking at a monkey."

Aimee begin to shuffle aimlessly on the porch, I could see her struggling to keep her hands from folding into clenched fists.

"Now Chesterfield, I thought we had all come to an agreement. We Saurians would protect this disgusting run-down little plot of land you call a town, and in return, you all would pay a fair and reasonable tax to us as compensation. The only stipulation being that we never have to look at your stupid little monkey faces in the process. Is that not what we agreed?"

"It is." By now Aimee's chin was nearly on her chest, and she craned her neck hard to the right, desperate to hold in a very apparent and very visible rage. This display seemed to delight Malazaar to no end, his reptilian face showed unmistakable signs of joy.

"Brothers!" he called out to the other lizard-men, who were currently dumping their collected taxes into a horse-drawn cart that they had brought along with them. They stopped their work, and with more reptilian grins made their way closer to both Malazaar and Aimee. "Ms. Chesterfield here was late with her tax, broke the one stipulation in our agreement and as a result, we have a monkey in our midst." The lizard-men begin to let out a sound that was an unnerving combination hissing and chuckling as they moved closer to the porch.

"This is bad, this is very very bad," Thomas whispered into the window sill.

"Why what's happening, what's going to happen?" As if I hadn't seen enough, Thomas and his mysterious and ominous muttering were about to send me spinning into a panic attack.

"The Saurians mainly come to take our food, our water, our wine, but sometimes they like to entertain themselves at our expense. They're aggressive and violent, and things usually don't go well for whoever they choose to be the focus of their attention. Malazaar can be especially nasty, and he's always had it in for my sister."

Malazaar swung a heavy leg around from the far side of his horse, and his back turned to us momentarily as he dismounted. He was draped in dark brown cloths, a tunic of some sort covered his shoulders and trousers of similar fabric hung loosely from his waist, most of his scales were covered except for lean muscular arms and his clawed lizard feet which themselves were bare and open. A long green tail swooshed back and forth from underneath his tunic. At Malazaar side, I noticed what for a moment looked like coils of rope, but upon closer inspection, I could see that it was actually a whip, interwoven strands of tightly braided leather, it almost gave off the impression of a second tail. But it was when Malazaar's feet hit the ground, and I saw what was strapped across his back that I truly felt the sting of surprise. He had a rifle. Not like the one I was holding, no, a much older version, a repeater rifle from the looks of it. My eyes scanned the other lizard-men, they were all wearing similar dark brown tunics, but now that I knew to look for it, it was not difficult to find, each of them had a strap across their chest and peeking out from behind their shoulders was the muzzle of another repeater rifle.

"They have guns?" I asked.

"Yes," Thomas replied, "Real guns, not like that hunk of junk you're holding." Thomas nodded down the piece of Huu-Mann tech I was still holding but still kept his eyes glued to the window.

Outside, Malazaar was approaching the porch, he reached down to his waist and uncoiled the whip, the length of it unfurled hitting the ground and curling through the dirt like a live snake.

"Ms. Chesterfield, your taxes were late,"

"They weren't late. I had two sacks of food on the porch before you arrived. As instr-"

"And you were on the porch along with them! The instructions are clear! Two Bags of Food, to bags of clothing, two barrels of water, two barrels of wine! Left in front of the door of every home occupied by an ape for quick and simple collection!"

Malazaar was screaming at this point, his hiss growl and roar all evident and echoing throughout the town. "You are on the porch, you have slowed down the collection of the taxes, you have hindered us in our duty! You have broken the agreement! And now I want to know what plan to do to make amends?!" Malazaar cracked the whip the sound of which seemed to put an exclamation point on the end of his statement. Thomas and I jumped in unison.

Aimee stood steadfast; her chin once again held skyward. She said nothing.

"You arrogant monkeys have always made me sick!" Malazaar moved liked lightning and flailed the whip forward, the leather coiled latched itself around Aimee's neck, and at that moment Malazaar yanked down, and Aimee came flying off of the porch landing face first in the dirt.

"Aimee!" Thomas yelled from the window. At the sound of his voice, Malazaar looked up to the window with fire and glee in his large yellow eyes. His lizard lips were pulled back into a smile and as soon as I saw it. I bolted.

Episode 4: Ancient Science and Antique Weaponry

I fled from the window with a speed I didn't know I had. Within seconds I was in the kitchen. My eyes darted in every direction. I spotted the back door, which I made a mental note of not noticing before. No surprise there, considering as of late there seemed to be a large number of items that I failed to see on the first go around. To the left of the door was a long wooden table and to the right, the food pantry, with the open crate still laid out on the floor in front of it.

I ran to the open crate grabbing up an armful of the old Huu-Mann tech guns and then dumped the entire haul on the large table along with the one that I had been carrying already. I grabbed my original gun and hit a small switched labeled "engage." It was unresponsive. Which I expected. I flipped the rifle over in my hands, one... two times. There was information there, in my mind. In my frazzled broken mind, the images and vision that I had been having all afternoon came back in all the right pieces.

It was a Mark II, Electromagnetic Plasma Pulse Rifle, with a Ryden Quad-Carbon Fuel Cell as a power supply. This was good, Ryden Carbon Fuel Cells had a half-life of some 5,000 years, so the chances of it still holding a positive charge as opposed to simply exploding in my face were as high as I could hope for. I begin to dismantle the rifle. My hands seemed to move of their own accord, faster than I could think. The gun broke down easily, I removed the metallic outer casing along the barrel revealing two parallel rails with half of an inch of open space between them. I pulled the two rails in opposite directions and the separated with little resistance. Beneath each of them was an additional metal rod wrapped tightly in thin copper wire, one of them was blackened and charred. Bad coil. I grabbed another one of the rifles and took it apart as well swapping out its good coil for my bad one. I did the same thing for three other bad parts on my gun, the heat transducer, the nitrogen coolant core, and bell switch all had to be replaced. I put the rifle back together and slapped the fuel cell into place. I hit the engage switch once again. A power indicator light blinked to life. The entire repair to two minutes. I looked back over to the crate and saw a small "L" shaped chunk of metal. An energy pistol. They had energy pistols too.

I grabbed my guns and ran back into the living room. Thomas was still at the window, tears streaming down his face, he looked back at my approach, slightly surprised to see me. He sniffled and wiped his face with his sleeve.

"What are you doing back here?" he asked through bloodshot red eyes.

"I'm going to go help your sister," I responded.

"You're what? No, you can't!" he hopped off of his crate and ran to block the door.

"What do you mean? Your sister needs help."

"No, you can't go out there. Yes, they'll hurt her, but if you go out there and try and stop them, they'll kill you and her."

Through the door, we heard another crack of the whip and an uproarious bout of laughter from the lizard-men. Both Thomas and I ran to the window, Aimee was in the dirt on all fours, hacking and coughing as if she was having a hard time breathing. She was covered in dirt, the shoulder of her dressed was ripped, and she was bleeding from a small cut above her eye.

"What is it that they say, brothers, Monkey See, Monkey Do!" Malazaar cracked the whip again. "Well Monkey, stand up."

Aimee attempted to stand, but a swift kick to the midsection sent her back to the dirt. The lizard-men burst out laughing once again. At that I sprinted toward the door, Thomas called after me, but I didn't slow down. I couldn't. Some unseen force pulled me forward, compelled me to act. There was no way I could sit inside that house and watch as they beat and humiliate the person who had just saved my life. I didn't know who I was, But I know I was not that.

I burst through the front door plasma rifle in hand, and a resonating ping let me know that the weapon was fully charged.

"Leave her alone!" I screamed upon stepping out onto the porch the rifle shouldered and pointed directly at Malazaar. The lizard-men froze momentarily, not really sure what to make of me. They looked at me, then looked at the plasma rifle and then looked down at Aimee, and then they all burst out laughing. "I'm not kidding!" I screamed trying as best as I could to not sound afraid. "This is a Mark II Electromagnetic Plasma Pulse Rifle it uses rail technology to launch a super-heated energy projectile up to 8,000 feet per second. And that energy will do inconceivable damage to any and all biological and non-biological matter that it comes in contact with."

The lizard-men paused again… and then once again burst out into fits of laughter.

"Listen here monkey-man."

"I am an Ape!" I cut Malazaar off mid-speech. "We are Apes! Not monkeys. The term monkey is rude and offensive. Do not say it anymore!" I spoke without thinking, purely reactionary, purely emotional. Emotions I didn't know that I had. "Aimee… Aimee come on back inside." I refuse to take my eye or my gun off Malazaar. Aimee stood to her feet, dusted herself off as best she could and began walking toward the porch.

Malazaar roared, he screamed and growled and hissed. He spoke in a language that may have been Saurian or may have been the same old language we had been speaking all along, I can't be sure. I couldn't tell you a word he said. My heart was beating too loud to hear anything. Blood was rushing in my ears and time seemed to slow to a crawl. The experience was surreal. The entire day had been surreal, but this particular moment more than all others had felt like a living dream. Aimee kept walking toward me. Malazaar kept screaming. The surrounding lizard-men seemed to be preparing their rifles, and for a moment I thought to myself, maybe it would have been better if I had simply died of thirst and starvation in the middle of nowhere as opposed to dying in a firefight with lizard-men in the middle of nowhere. Then there was a small thought in the back of my mind that whispered: "I'd rather not die at all."

Aimee stepped pass me, and up on to the porch, this seemed to enrage Malazaar beyond all belief. His head fin was fully erect, and the bright multi-colored membrane was rippling through an assortment of different shades. He cocked back his whip, I imagine to grab Aimee by the neck and pull her back to the ground, either that, or he was planning to use it to slash me across the face, it was hard to tell considering that I hadn't been exactly listening to his swear-filled rant. His whip arm raised high into the air, and I caught the words "Stupid monkey," and then there was a clearly audible warbling sound, the distinct smell of ozone, and a small visual cue of what looked like a bright purple bolt of encapsulated lightning arc out and shoot past Malazaar. Leaving in its wake a very large and perfectly round hole where his chest had been. The space in itself was empty but from the top of the hole dripped small amounts of blood from what few parts of the wound that had not been immediately cauterized by the heat of the blast. Malazaar looked down at the hole where his chest had been, his whip arm still high in the air. He looked back up at me and the now gently smoking barrel of the plasma rifle I was holding. The interior of the barrel radiated a soft purple glow, the same color of the energy bolt it had just fired.

"You have mastered Huu-Mann tech?" he muttered, sounding more than a little confused, his already lispy speech was now further colluded with what sounded like a drunken slur, and then there was another warbling sound and Malazaar's head exploded. I looked down at my plasma rifle suspecting that it may have malfunctioned and misfired, as I knew I had only pulled the trigger once for the chest shot. But then a receding hum of a recharging battery made me look over my shoulder to see Aimee holding a gun. An energy pistol, I had repaired it as well and jammed it in the back of my pants as a backup. Aimee must have seen it and... and decided to put it to use.

"The Apes have slain Malazaar!" shouted one of the remaining lizard-men one of the fiery orange ones. He too had a head fin, though his was much smaller in size then Malazaar's had been, yet and still I assume that made him next in line to lead. Either way, he choose to act first. He pulled the trigger of his old repeater rifle, and the front end of the barrel exploded with smoke and fire, his shot went wide, and large splinters of wood ripped themselves from a beam that was helping to hold up the porch roof. A few feet to the left and the shot would have gone clean through my head. Needless to say, I immediately threw myself face first into the dirt and scrambled behind a heavy wooden rain barrel that sat in front of the porch. Within seconds of the first shot, a hail of gunfire rained in my direction. The wood barrel that I was using as cover chipped and splintered as it was pelted by small but deadly fragments hot metal that flew through the air at speeds faster than the eyes could see.

After a few seconds the gunfire stopped and in that brief window, I was joined in my hiding place behind the barrel by another figure. It was Aimee. She landed on the ground next to me with a thud. And just like that, the gunfire began again.

"Mr. Simon, I'd like to thank you for coming to my aid." She spoke as if we weren't pinned down by giant bipedal lizards hell-bent on killing us.

"Well… um, it was the least I could do… you saved my life first after all." With every gunshot that ricocheted off the barrel, I winced and jumped, constantly assuming the next bullet would be the one that would find its mark.

"Well, I thank you all the same. Also, my Huu-Mann tech stopped working, did I do something to break it." I looked at the energy pistol she was still holding, the charge light was blinking yellow.

"No, that one just didn't have as long to charge as mine did, it only stored up enough power for one shot, it should be ready to go when all of these lights turn green, it needs about another minute."

"Oh," she said, then she looked at me and then down at the energy rifle. I was holding it as if it was a loaf of bread and not a highly technologically advanced weapon. "So… are you going to just hold that thing or…"

"Oh yeah," I said finally catching the hint. I held the Plasma rifle up with one hand and blindly fired over the barrel, squeezing the trigger three times in quick succession. The gunfire paused for a moment, and as it did, I popped up, steadied myself against the barrel and let off three more burst. I hit the orange lizard with the head fin and one of the brown ones before I even knew what happen. The remaining two froze, looked at one another and considered what to do next. Continue to fight or make a run for it. Before they could make a decision, Aimee popped up from behind the barrel with the energy pistol and vaporized the chest of one of the two remaining lizard-men.

The last Saurian stared at his surrounding with a combination of awe and disbelief. He stumbled backward tripped over his own tail and fell bottom first into the dirt. Desperate to escape but cautious not to take his eyes off of us for a moment, he scuttled backward in much the same way I had done when I woke up for the first time in the home of Aimee and Thomas. The crab walking was apparently not expedient enough for the Saurian, and he turned and began scrambling away on all fours. His tail whipped back and forth voraciously as his arms his legs propelled him across the ground with a speed that was still surprisingly fast even though his movements seemed unexpectedly natural. What moments ago had been a terrifying monster had now become a nothing more than a lowly lizard scurrying across the desert sand.

The Saurian made it to the nearest horse, climbed into the saddle and slapped the reigns hard urging it to sprint west, back into the direction from which they had come. Aimee raised the energy pistol, the gun pointed in the direction of the fleeing Saurian. I reached across her, placed a hand on the weapon and lowered it.

"If he gets away he will tell the others," she said. "They will return, and there will be even more of them at least a dozen next time." As she spoke apes from the other homes and buildings began to peek out of their doors and pour into the street. There were dozens of them. The town was full of Ape-men, women, and children.

"Perhaps," I said quietly watching the mounted lizard-man gallop away. "But if they return, you all will be ready for them."

Episode 5: Wasteland of Sand and Secrets

Mr. Chesterfield, Aimee and Thomas's father, had been busy. In addition to the one open crate, the kitchen pantry held two more heavy wooden boxes full of non-functioning plasma weapons. Over a period of two days, I was able to salvage from them, six fully functioning rifles and two more energy pistols. Aimee distributed the weapons to the most capable individuals within the town, and I instructed them in the basic understanding of their use.

"Simon," Aimee spoke my name now as if we were old friends, We stood on her porch watching as the townsfolk went about their daily chores, two apes holding Plasma Rifles patrolled the cities perimeter at all times, just in case the Saurian decided to return. "Will you… do you, plan on staying here, in the town? Everyone has taken quite a liking to you, and you could be of great help."

I shook my head, "I don't think so… There is still... there's still so much I don't know, about my past, about who I am. I think the answers are out there." I looked up toward a sea of rolling sand dunes, to the east, "In the desert, in that facility your father found, something tells me that's where I'll find the answers I'm looking for."

"I imagined you'd say as much, You know it is funny, I have only known you for the briefest of moments, and yet in so many ways, you remind me of my father. Simon, if you find the facility can you, will you please look for my father, could you let him know Thomas and I are waiting for him to return."

"I will," I said solemnly.

"I-I have something to show you."

I followed Aimee around to the back of their house where an assortment broken machines lay scattered about. Aimee walked up to canvas tarp that covered something large, it was almost at chest height and easily six feet long. In one flourish she ripped the tarp away revealing a massive machine that sat on two large black wheels. In the middle of it, between the wheels and on top of the heavy machinery was what looked similar to the Saurian horse's saddle, only instead of reigns, there were a set of metal bars that protruded in opposing directions.

"It's a Solar Bike!" I said with obvious surprise and excitement.

"As far as Huu-Mann Tech goes this was my father's prized possession, he assumed it was for traveling quickly over long distances, but he couldn't figure out how to get it to work, maybe you can."

I went to work immediately using whatever I could salvage from the other machines in the Chesterfields junk pile. Over the course of another day, with Thomas looking over my shoulder the entire time, I managed to get the sun-powered Solar Bike up and running again. I received a week's worth of rations from Aimee, bread, cheese, and some dried meats, I placed them along with a change of clothes in the saddlebags of the bike. Aimee also handed me one of the energy pistols along with one other item.

"You should take this, it may be of some use." She handed me a coil of braided leather straps, the leather whip that had at one time been in the hand of the Saurian who terrorized their humble little town.

"You want me to take this? Wouldn't you rather, I don't know, destroy it or something?"

"No, I think it would be better used in the hands of someone like you, who knows, if your Huu-Mann Tech needs to recharge or if that funny brain of yours can't remember how to fix something, this may come in handy." She smiled at me, and I couldn't help but smile back. "Malazaar called it the Dragon's Tail, I guess you've got a monkey tail now."

I chuckled, "Aimee thank you for everything, I promise I'll find your father and bring him back, that's the least I could do-" She cut me off mid-speech and pressed her lips against mine. We stood frozen in this position for a moment that seemed to stretch into forever, a forever that lasted right up until I heard a small voice cut in and ask.

"What are you two doing?"

I pulled myself away from Aimee to find Thomas standing a short distance away with a tight-eyed grimace of suspicion and accusation across his face.

"Oh, nothing" I shuffled about nervously under his tiny accusatory eyes, "I was just… Aimee and I were just saying goodbye."

"Why? You're coming back, aren't you? You're not leaving for forever."

"No, no you're right," I smiled, "I'll be back."

"Well alright then, no need to say goodbye, just see ya later."

My smile grew bigger. "You're right," I hopped onto the back of the Solar Bike and pressed the ignition button, the engine hummed into life. I looked back, winked at Thomas and then nodded at Aimee. "See ya later," I said.

I twisted the accelerator on the handlebar and sped off into the desert, one word in the forefront of my mind, Huu-Mann, no not Huu-Mann, Human. Yes in the desert, I would find it. The secret of these Ancient Humans and with it the secret to my own identity.

The End.

Afterword…

This concludes A Poor Excuse for a Book, I hope you have enjoyed reading it as much as I have enjoyed writing it.

Thanks,

-Nate

www.ingramcontent.com/pod-product-compliance
Lightning Source LLC
Chambersburg PA
CBHW050137110726

47898CB00008B/2572